Usborne Fairy Tales for Bedtime

Retold by Rosie Dickins

Illustrated by Nathalie Ragondet

Contents

5

Cinderella

based on a French tale by Charles Perrault

15

Goldilocks and the Three Bears

based on a tale by the Brothers Grimm

23

Jack and the Beanstalk

based on an English fairytale

31

Rapunzel

based on a tale by the Brothers Grimm

39

Puss in Boots

based on an Italian fairytale

47

Snow White and the Seven Dwarfs

based on a tale by the Brothers Grimm

57

Hansel and Gretel

based on a tale by the Brothers Grimm

67

Little Red Riding Hood

based on a tale by the Brothers Grimm

75

The Elves and the Shoemaker

based on a tale by the Brothers Grimm

83

Aladdin and the Magic Lamp

based on a tale from the *Arabian Nights*

93

The Three Wishes

based on an English fairytale

Cinderella

Once upon a time, there was
a beautiful young girl named
Ella. But everyone called
her Cinderella...

...because while the rest of her family slept in soft feather beds, she had to huddle by the fireplace in the kitchen and wake covered in ash and cinders.

Cinderella's mother had died years before, and her father (who was rarely home) had married again. His new wife made Cinderella scrub and sweep and cook and clean. But she lavished every luxury on her own two girls – who were as ugly as Cinderella was beautiful.

One day, an invitation arrived which made Cinderella's stepmother shriek with excitement.

"The prince is holding a ball!" she cried. "And we're invited." At once, she and her daughters began discussing dresses and shoes, and how to impress a prince.

"Please may I go too?" begged Cinderella.

"You?" laughed her stepmother. "Just look at you, covered in cinders like a kitchen maid! They'd never let *you* into the palace."

Over the following days, Cinderella's stepmother summoned the most fashionable dressmakers and hairdressers, to make the ugly sisters look slightly less ugly. It wasn't easy.

Finally, the big night arrived. The sisters and their mother left in a swish of finery, and Cinderella was alone in an empty house.

"I *wish* I could go to the ball," she sighed. Hardly had the words left her lips than there was a tap at the door. There stood an old lady leaning on a silver stick. Cinderella had never seen her before, but she seemed to know Cinderella.

"Hello dear," she said. "I'm your fairy godmother and you *shall* go to the ball! First, you need a coach. Can you bring me a pumpkin?"

Cinderella was too astonished to ask why. She ran to pick a pumpkin from the garden.

Her godmother waved the stick. There was a shower of stars, so bright that Cinderella had to blink. When she looked again, the pumpkin had become a round, golden coach. She gasped.

"Now the coachman and horses," her godmother went on. "I think you'll find a lizard and four mice in the garden..." Another wave, and there was a coachman dressed all in green, and four handsome white horses.

"And your dress," she added. With a final wave, Cinderella's ragged old clothes became a glittering ballgown, while delicate glass slippers sparkled on her feet.

Cinderella spun around in delight. "Oh thank you, godmother," she cried.

"Now remember," said her godmother, as Cinderella stepped into the golden coach. "My magic will wear off at midnight. You must leave before then!"

"I will," promised Cinderella.

The palace was ablaze with lights when Cinderella arrived. As she entered, a hush fell. No one had ever seen anyone so beautiful. Shyly, the prince came over and asked her to dance. Cinderella's glass slippers tinkled lightly on the dance floor as she and the prince whirled and twirled together.

They were having so much fun, she almost forgot her godmother's warning – until a clock began to strike...

"Midnight!" she gasped. She gathered up her skirts and dashed for the door.

"Don't go," called the prince, racing after her. But he was too late. She had vanished – except for one sparkling glass slipper. Gently, he picked it up.

"I'm going to find the girl who fits this," he announced boldly. "And then I'm going to ask her to marry me!"

The very next day, the prince and his servants carried the slipper from house to house. Everyone tried it, from haughty princesses to humble house maids, but it would fit no one.

Cinderella's ugly sisters tried it too, but their feet were far too big and clumpy. Then a shy, cinder-covered figure stepped forward.

"It can't be *hers*," sneered the sisters. "She wasn't even at the ball."

"I want *everyone* to try," insisted the prince, gazing hopefully at the girl. Was it his imagination, or was there something familiar about her...? He held his breath as, daintily, she lifted her foot. The slipper was a perfect fit!

"I knew I'd find you," he cried joyfully, sweeping Cinderella into his arms.

"My prince," she laughed, hugging him right back.

At that moment, there was a tap at the door. It was Cinderella's fairy godmother. "Time for a little more magic," she said, with a smile.

She waved her wand and Cinderella's dusty dress was transformed into a dazzling wedding gown – and there was a golden coach to carry the smiling couple back to the palace, where they lived happily ever after.

Cinderella's stepmother and sisters were less happy. "It's all your fault," the stepmother grumbled at her daughters, "for having such big feet!"

Goldilocks and the Three Bears

Goldilocks had pretty golden curls
and a sweet-as-sugar smile. She
looked like an angel. Unfortunately,
she didn't behave like one...

"Greedy Goldilocks," her mother sighed, as she caught her in the kitchen. "Those cakes are for later! Put them back. Why don't you play outside?" she went on. "Just don't go into the forest. It's full of bears!"

Goldilocks didn't answer. She was already dancing out of the door.

Leaves rustled and birds sang as she skipped along the path to the forest. "I can't see any bears," she laughed, looking around. Between the trees, she spied a pretty wooden cottage.

"Who lives here?" she wondered, skipping up to the door. *Rat-a-tat-tat!* No one came, so she pushed her way in.

"Ooh, something smells good," she thought. On a table sat three bowls of creamy porridge.

Goldilocks grabbed the biggest bowl and scooped up a steamy spoonful. "Oof!" she spluttered. "Too hot." She reached for the middle-sized bowl. "Ugh! Too cold." But the littlest bowl was... "*Mmm,* just right." Goldilocks gobbled it all up.

Beside the table were three painted wooden chairs. Goldilocks clambered onto the biggest chair. "Oof, too hard." Next she flopped onto the middle-sized chair. "Ugh, too soft." But the littlest chair was... "*Mmm,* just right."

At least, it *was* until its little legs gave way beneath her. *CRASH!*

"Ow! Now where will I sit?" she moaned, brushing off the splinters.

A curtain hung across one corner. Behind it stood three comfy-looking beds. She bounced on the biggest bed. "Oof, too hard!" She sank into the middle-sized bed. "Ugh, too soft." But the littlest bed was... "*Mmm*, just right."

Feeling sleepy after all the porridge, she pulled the covers up to her chin and dozed off. She was snoozing so soundly, she didn't hear the door open and three sets of paws come padding inside. But she jolted awake when three voices suddenly boomed out.

"Who's been eating *my* porridge?" growled a big, deep voice.

"Who's been eating *my* porridge?" gasped a middling sort of voice.

"Who's been eating *my* porridge?" squeaked a little baby voice. "And look, they've eaten it all up!"

"*Uh-oh*," thought Goldilocks, peeking around the curtain. "Bears!"

"Who's been sitting in *my* chair?" growled the great big bear.

"Who's been sitting in *my* chair?" gasped the middle-sized bear.

"Who's been sitting in *my* chair?" squeaked the little baby bear. "Look, they've broken it!"

The three bears turned towards the beds... Goldilocks dived under the covers, trembling. "I hope they don't see me!"

"Who's been sleeping in *my* bed?" growled the great big bear.

"Who's been sleeping in *my* bed?" gasped the middle-sized bear.

"Who's been sleeping in *my* bed?" squealed the little baby bear. "Look, she's still in it!"

Goldilocks shrieked and flung off the bedcovers. She raced out of the cottage and all the way home, as fast as her legs could carry her. And she was never, or *almost* never, naughty again.

Jack and the Beanstalk

There was once a poor boy
named Jack whose mother
sent him to market to sell
their cow.

So off Jack strolled, leading the cow, when he bumped into a stranger.

"That's a fine animal," said the stranger, patting the cow's milky-white flank. "I'll give you a handful of beans for her."

"Beans?" laughed Jack. "She's worth more than that!"

"Ah, but these are magic beans," promised the man, winking. And somehow, Jack found himself nodding...

"Silly boy," cried his mother when he got back. "Now we have no cow and no money!" She flung the beans out of the window and went sadly to bed.

The next morning, Jack woke to find his room flooded with green light. Leaves and tendrils filled the window. "A giant beanstalk!" he gasped, gazing up. The end disappeared into the clouds.

"I wonder what's up there?" thought Jack – and he began to climb. Up and up, until the ground dropped away and his cottage looked like a toy. Up into the clouds...

The beanstalk ended outside a towering castle, with its huge oak door ajar. Jack slipped through.

Inside stood a table and chair as big as
a house. A whole tree was burning in the
fireplace, and a whole ox was roasting over it.

"This must be a giant's castle!" Jack gasped.
The floor began to shake. "Uh-oh, footsteps."
He ducked behind a table leg.

"*Fee-fi-fo-fum*," roared the giant, stomping
in. "I smell the blood of a little man." He licked
his lips greedily. "And
I *eat* little men for
breakfast!"

Behind the table,
Jack shivered. The
giant looked around
but didn't spy him.
So he grabbed the ox
instead, and crunched
it up in two bites.

"Now, where's that hen?" he muttered. He picked up a basket and roughly shook it, until a hen with shining golden feathers fell out.

"Lay!" he snapped. With much flapping and fluttering, the hen laid a heavy golden egg.

"Wow," thought Jack. "That's real gold!"

"Where's my harp?" the giant went on. He opened a cupboard and yanked out a harp with shining golden strings. "Play!" And the harp began to play all by itself. It played such a sweet, restful tune that the giant was soon snoring peacefully.

"What treasures," thought Jack. "If we had those, Mother would never be short of money again."

Quickly, quietly, Jack tiptoed over and seized the hen and the harp. But as he crept away, he stumbled and the harp let out a loud *twang.* "Oh no!"

Behind him came an ear-splitting roar. The giant had woken up.

Jack didn't hesitate. He raced to the beanstalk and slid down as fast as he could, the giant clambering clumsily after him.

As soon as Jack reached the bottom, he seized a hatchet and chopped through the stalk. The giant was only halfway down. He fell to earth with a giant-sized thump, and that was the end of him.

But Jack and his mother lived happily with the golden hen and the golden harp and, as they soon had lots of golden eggs to sell, they never wanted for anything again.

Rapunzel

O nce upon a time, a young mother fell ill. Only one thing could cure her – a herb named rapunzel.

But it was cold
midwinter and there was
none to be had, except
in the garden of a wicked
witch. Bravely, her husband
crept into the garden to pick a leaf...

As the stem snapped, he heard a shriek.
"Stop, thief!" It was the witch. "How dare you
steal my plant? You shall pay with your life!"

"I'm sorry," he pleaded. "It was for my wife,
she's very ill. Please, she's expecting a baby..."

The witch gave a nasty grin. "I'll take the
baby as payment then."

Sadly, the man bowed his head. He had no
choice. The witch was too powerful.

The baby, when she came, was a beautiful
rosy-cheeked girl. She had scarcely drawn her
first breath when there was a rap at the door.

The witch had come to claim her. "I'll call her Rapunzel," she cackled, as she took the tiny bundle away, "in memory of our bargain."

So Rapunzel grew up with the witch – who guarded her jealously. She kept her locked in a tower with no door. The only way in or out was to climb, but the sides of the tower were as slippery as glass and cruel thorn bushes grew all around.

Rapunzel had thick, golden hair which grew and grew, and was never cut. When the witch came, she would call up: "Rapunzel, Rapunzel, let down your hair."

Then Rapunzel would let her hair tumble to the ground, and the witch would climb up it.

One day, a prince was riding by the tower when he spied Rapunzel, combing her hair by her window. She was so beautiful, he lost his heart to her in an instant. And Rapunzel, who had never seen a man before, was equally charmed.

Quickly, she let down her hair. Boldly, the prince climbed up. They talked and laughed for hours. And by sunset, they had vowed to marry.

"But you must leave before the witch comes," warned Rapunzel. "Or she'll kill you."

"I'll be back soon," promised the prince. "And then we'll escape together!"

When the witch returned, she sniffed suspiciously. "A man has been here," she hissed. "But you won't see him again!" She chopped off Rapunzel's beautiful hair and locked her in a cupboard. And then the witch waited...

Before long, there came a whisper. "Rapunzel, Rapunzel, let down your hair." The golden tresses tumbled down and the prince climbed up – only to find the witch holding the other end.

"You'll never see your darling again," she cackled, holding up a claw-like hand and mouthing a spell. The prince's world suddenly grew dark. The witch had blinded him. Then he felt her cold fingers on his chest, trying to push him back out of the window.

"No," he cried, thinking of the deadly drop onto the thorns below. He fought blindly, and managed to throw the witch off balance...

She teetered...

and tottered...

and fell through the window herself. There was a loud shriek – and a sudden silence.

"Well, she won't trouble us again," sighed the prince in relief. "Rapunzel?"

"Here," answered a soft voice. The prince felt his way over to the cupboard and unlocked it, and Rapunzel rushed into his arms. Tears of joy streamed down her cheeks – and when her tears touched the prince's eyes, he found he could see again.

He blinked and smiled. "We're free," he told her gently. "Come with me, and we can live happily ever after together."

And they did.

Puss in Boots

There was once a poor miller's
boy who found himself alone
in the world, with no family and no
job, and only a large stripy cat
for company.

The boy's name was Peppo. "Well Puss," he sighed, stroking the cat's soft, tawny fur. "I've no work and almost no money. What will we do together?"

"We will do very well, if you will trust me," purred Puss.

"You can talk!" exclaimed Peppo.

"Oh yes," purred Puss, smiling. "And much more besides. You will soon see, if you will just buy me a new suit and boots."

So Peppo turned out his pockets... With his last few coins, he bought a little red velvet jacket, with hat and boots – and very handsome Puss looked in them.

Puss then caught a couple of fine, fat rabbits and took them to the King. "A present from the Marquis of Catanza," he mewed.

The next day, he took two gleaming silver salmon. "From the Marquis of Catanza," he mewed again.

On the third day, it was a pair of plump golden pheasants...

"Who is this Marquis who keeps sending me gifts?" asked the King curiously.

"You don't know the Marquis?" gasped Puss. "A man famed for his wit, wisdom and wealth?"

"Er, no," admitted the King. "But I'd love to meet him. Can you bring him to the palace?"

Puss smiled.

"What have you done?" moaned Peppo when Puss returned with the invitation. "I'm no marquis!" He looked sadly at his old, patched clothes. "And I can't meet the King like this."

"Don't worry," said Puss. "I'll come up with something. Why don't you go for a swim in the river while I think about it."

So Peppo went for a swim. While he was splashing in the sunshine, Puss took all his clothes and hid them under a rock. Then he ran to the palace, mewing loudly.

"Help, help! Thieves have attacked the Marquis and stolen his clothes, and thrown him in the river to drown!"

The King immediately sent his soldiers and servants to the rescue, along with a suit of his own clothes for Peppo.

So Peppo arrived at the palace dressed like
a king – and looking as handsome as a king, too.
The King's daughter, Princess Perla, blushed
with delight whenever she saw him.

The King gave a great feast to celebrate
Peppo's visit. After all the food, Puss suggested
they go for a walk. "So you can
see my master's castle,"
he mewed.

"What are you doing?"
hissed Peppo.

Puss just winked and
scampered ahead.

Now, it happened that
there was a castle not far
from the King's palace and
it belonged to a fearsome ogre.

Puss ran straight up to the ogre.

"People say you can change shape," he mewed boldly. "But I don't believe it!"

"Then watch," snarled the ogre. And he turned into a great big grizzly bear. "Grrrrrr!"

"Not bad," admitted Puss. "But I bet you can't go as small as a mouse."

"Watch," growled the bear, shrinking...

Puss grinned – and pounced.

When the King and Peppo arrived, Puss was calmly cleaning his whiskers. "Welcome to my master's castle," he purred. The King was very impressed.

Now it was Peppo's turn to give a feast. He and Perla danced all night and by morning, they were engaged to be married.

So Peppo and Perla lived happily ever after with Puss by their fireside, and Puss never chased another mouse again, except for fun.

Snow White and the Seven Dwarfs

Princess Snow White was
the prettiest child you ever
saw, with hair as black as ebony,
lips as red as roses and skin as
white as snow.

As she grew up, she grew ever more beautiful, while her stepmother, the Queen, grew ever more jealous.

Each day, the Queen gazed coldly into her mirror. "Mirror, mirror, on the wall, who is the fairest of them all?"

"You, my Queen," replied the mirror... until one day it said instead, "Snow White."

The Queen scowled. "*I* must be the fairest," she hissed. And she sent a huntsman to take the princess into the forest and kill her.

But the old huntsman took pity on Snow White and left her unhurt among the trees. "Don't go home," he warned, "or the Queen will have you killed."

"Where shall I go?" she wondered sadly.

After much walking, she came to a cottage. There was no one at home, but inside stood seven little beds in a row, and a long, low table set for seven dinners.

By now she was so tired, she crept in and fell asleep by the fire – and that is how the seven dwarfs who lived in the cottage found her, when they came home.

The dwarfs were very surprised to find Snow White, and even more surprised to hear her story. "You poor thing," they cried. "You must stay here with us. You can mind the house while we go out to work, and we will have dinner together each evening."

"Oh, thank you," sighed Snow White.

"Be careful though," warned the dwarfs. "Your stepmother may come after you, even here. Don't let anyone in while we're away!"

Meanwhile, the Queen was gazing into her mirror again. "*Now* who is the fairest?"

"Oh Queen, you are fair, indeed it's true, But Snow White is fairer still than you."

"But she's dead!" wailed the Queen, with a scowl. "Isn't she?"

In reply, the mirror showed her a picture of Snow White and the dwarfs, sitting happily down to dinner.

The Queen howled. "That lying huntsman! I'll have to kill her myself."

The next morning, Snow White had barely cleared the breakfast things when there was a tap at the door. She opened it a crack and saw an old woman.

"Pretty things to buy," croaked the woman, holding up a glittering silver belt.

"I can't let anyone in," said Snow White.

"Then come outside," said the woman.

Snow White didn't want to be rude, so she stepped out. The woman slipped the belt around her waist and pulled, hard. Snow White gasped and fell to the ground, unable to breathe.

When the dwarfs came home, she was still lying there. Quickly, they loosened the belt, and Snow White coughed and sat up.

"Next time, don't even open the door," they told her.

The next day, there was another tap. "I can't open the door," said Snow White.

"Then open the window," came the reply.

Snow White did – and saw an old woman holding out a silver comb. "Try it, dearie."

It looked so pretty, Snow White couldn't resist. But as soon as she touched it, she fell to the floor, for it was poisoned.

When the dwarfs came home, they pulled it away, and Snow White sat up. "Don't accept *anything* from anyone," they said sternly.

The next day, someone tapped again. "Who is it?" Snow White called cautiously.

"Just an old apple-seller."

Snow White peeked out and saw an old woman with a basket of shiny apples.

"These are delicious," she cackled, holding out a glossy green apple with one rosy red cheek. "Look." And she took a bite from the green side.

"It must be all right if *she's* eating it," thought Snow White. She took a bite of the red side – and fell lifeless to the floor. The old woman threw back her hood and laughed. It was the Queen, and the red apple was poison.

This time, the dwarfs could not revive Snow White. With heavy hearts they made a glass case for her, so as not to hide her beauty, and left her in a quiet part of the forest.

A few weeks later, a prince was riding by when he saw Snow White lying peacefully under the glass, as beautiful as ever. In that instant, the prince fell utterly in love.

He leaped down, pushed aside the lid and lifted her into his arms. As he stood up, he stumbled over a tree root – and with the jolt, a piece of apple flew out of her mouth.

As soon as the apple passed her lips, the poison ceased to work. Snow White coughed prettily and opened her eyes. She blushed to find herself in the arms of a dashing prince.

"You're alive," he cried happily, while the dwarfs danced around in delight. "Will you marry me?"

"Oh yes," sighed Snow White, blushing even more.

So they were married, and all seven dwarfs came to the wedding.

Hansel and Gretel

H ansel and Gretel lived with
their father and stepmother
in a little wooden cottage on the
edge of an enormous forest.

The forest was so huge and so wild, Hansel
and Gretel had never seen most of it.
Each morning, their father set off
with his hatchet. Each evening,
he came home with bundles of
firewood to sell. But times were
hard and, try as he might, they
never had enough to eat.

Late one night, after Hansel
and Gretel had gone to bed, their stepmother
turned crossly to their father. "If it was just you
and me, we might manage," she snapped. "But
we can't feed two children as well! You'll have
to take them into the forest and leave them."

"No!" cried the woodcutter. But she
wouldn't listen. Hunger had hardened her
heart. She nagged and bullied, until reluctantly
he was forced to agree.

Hansel and Gretel were too hungry and worried to sleep. They had heard every word.

"What now, Hansel?" whispered Gretel.

"Don't worry, I've got a plan," he replied. He waited until everyone was asleep. Then, silently, he slipped outside and filled his pockets with pebbles.

In the morning, the woodcutter hugged his children and gave them each a little piece of bread. "Put on your coats," he said, sighing. "You're coming with me today."

He led them deep into the forest, along strange paths with many twists and turns. At each turn, Hansel lingered and secretly dropped a pebble to mark the way.

"Keep up, son," muttered his father.

Eventually they came to a clearing. "You stay here while I start chopping," said the woodcutter sadly. "I'll come and get you later."

Hansel and Gretel sat and waited. In the distance, they could hear the *thud-thud-thud* of the hatchet. Except it wasn't really a hatchet. The woodcutter had tied a branch so it thudded against a tree when the wind blew.

They sat until the sun began to sink. Gretel shivered. "Time to go home," said Hansel. And back they went, following the pebbles, until they reached the cottage.

"You're home!" cried the woodcutter gladly.

His wife scowled. As soon as the children were in bed, she turned on her husband. "You'll have to try again tomorrow!"

Again, Hansel and Gretel overheard.

"Don't worry," said Hansel. "I'll get some more pebbles." He waited until everyone was asleep, then tiptoed to the door... but it wouldn't open. His stepmother had locked it. "Never mind," he told himself bravely. "I'm sure I can find something else."

The next morning, the woodcutter kissed his children and divided the last little piece of bread between them.

"Put on your coats," he sighed. And off they went, into the forest... This time, Hansel had nothing in his pockets but bread. So he crumbled that, and dropped the crumbs to mark the way.

The woodcutter left them as before – and as before, they sat and waited for the end of the day. Then they got up to make their way home… only to find there were no crumbs to be seen! The forest birds had eaten every one.

"Perhaps I'll remember the way," thought Hansel. But he didn't. They wandered deeper and deeper into the trees, until they stumbled upon a small clearing.

"Look!" gasped Gretel. There, in the middle, stood a little house built of freshly baked gingerbread, with lollipop windows and sugar flowers around the door. It looked wonderful and it smelled even better.

Too hungry to think, they ran over and crammed their mouths with sweet, sticky handfuls. They ate and ate, until they could eat no more. And then they fell asleep.

Gretel was woken by a
sharp prod. It was a witch,
who had built the gingerbread
house to catch passing
children. "Get up, girl," she
snapped. "You're my servant now."

"Hey," called Hansel, trying to stand
up. His head hit something hard. "Ow!"
He was caught in a cage. "Let me out!"

The witch cackled. "You're not going
anywhere. Your sister is going to feed you up,
and then I'm going to eat you!"

Each day, she made Hansel hold out a
finger, so she could feel how fat he was. But he
soon realized that the witch, though powerful,
couldn't see very well. So he would hold out
a twig instead... "Why aren't you fatter?" she
would grumble, leaving him for another day.

One morning, the witch lost patience. "Open the oven," she shouted at Gretel. "The fire is lit and I'm hungry."

Gretel thought fast. "How does it open?"

"Like this, you silly girl," snapped the witch, bending down.

Quick as a flash, Gretel pushed her in and slammed the door – and that was the end of her. Then Gretel opened Hansel's cage and they set out for home, stopping only to fill a basket with gingerbread and take a purse of the witch's gold.

At last, to their delight, they found a familiar path. Then they saw their cottage. Their father was alone inside, for their step-mother had left. "I missed you so much," he sobbed, hugging them tightly.

With the gold, their worries were over – and they all lived happily ever after.

Little Red Riding Hood

Once there was a little girl, whose mother made her a cape and hood of soft, red cloth. She liked the cape so much and wore it so often, everyone began to call her Little Red Riding Hood.

One day, Little Red Riding Hood's mother asked her to take a cake to her grandmother, who lived on the other side of the forest. "Now be careful and stay on the path," she warned her daughter. "And don't talk to any wolves!"

Little Red Riding Hood set off happily. She was so busy singing to herself and picking flowers, she didn't notice a dark shape slinking through the shadows...

In the deepest, darkest part of the forest, an enormous wolf sprang out in front of her. "Where are you going, little girl?" he growled.

Little Red Riding Hood was so startled, she forgot her mother's words. "To visit my granny beyond the forest," she replied. "I'm taking her this cake."

The wolf had meant to eat up Little Red Riding Hood there and then, but now he had a better idea. "I'll eat the old lady first – and have this little girl and her cake for dessert!" With a sly smile, he ran off through the trees.

The wolf got to the house long before Little Red Riding Hood. He knocked impatiently on the door. *Rat-a-tat!*

"Who is it?" called a quavery old voice.

"Your little granddaughter, with a cake for you," he answered in a squeaky voice.

"Lift up the latch and come in."

The wolf bounded in and swallowed the grandmother whole – *gulp!*

Then he pulled her frilly cap over his big, hairy ears, tied her shawl around his huge, hairy shoulders, and jumped into her bed.

Soon, there was another knock at the door. *Rat-a-tat!* "Who is it?" quavered the wolf.

"Red Riding Hood, with a cake for you."

"Lift up the latch and come in."

Little Red Riding Hood pushed open the door – and stared. "Granny, what big *ears* you have," she exclaimed.

"All the better to hear you with," squeaked the wolf.

"Granny, what big *eyes* you have."

"All the better to see you with."

"Granny, what big *teeth* you have."

"All the better to eat you with!" snarled the wolf, jumping up and swallowing Little Red Riding Hood and the cake together – *gulp!*

Then the wolf yawned. After eating so much, he felt sleepy. So he flopped down on the bed and closed his eyes.

In a moment, he was snoring loudly – so loudly that a passing woodcutter heard him.

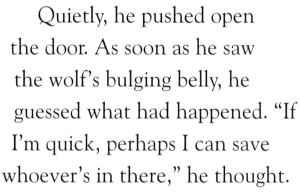

"What a racket," he muttered. "I'd better see if everything is all right."

Quietly, he pushed open the door. As soon as he saw the wolf's bulging belly, he guessed what had happened. "If I'm quick, perhaps I can save whoever's in there," he thought.

He tiptoed over to the bed and picked up a pair of scissors...

Snip, snip! He cut open the wolf's tummy and out sprang Little Red Riding Hood.

Snip, snip! Out tumbled her grandmother too.

"Can you find some stones?" the woodcutter asked Little Red Riding Hood. He put the stones in the wolf's tummy and sewed it up. Then they all crept softly away.

When the wolf woke, his tummy felt peculiar. "That old granny must have disagreed with me," he grumbled. "I'd better drink some water."

He ran to the river, the stones inside him rattling and rolling with every step. Then he leaned down to drink... but the stones were so heavy, he fell right in. *Splosh!* The rushing water swept him away and no one ever saw him again.

Little Red Riding Hood and her granny lived long and happily, thanks to the brave woodcutter. And Little Red Riding Hood never, ever talked to another wolf.

The Elves
and the
Shoemaker

There was once an old
shoemaker who fell on hard
times. He was so short of money,
he couldn't even afford to buy
any more leather...

All he had was a few scraps.

"Enough for a small pair,"
he decided, picking up
his scissors. *Snip, snip,
snippety-snip.* Carefully,
he began to cut out the
pieces. By the time he
finished, it was too dark to
stitch them together.

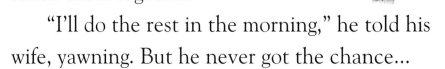

"I'll do the rest in the morning," he told his
wife, yawning. But he never got the chance...

When he woke the next day, the leather had
gone! In its place was a pair of shiny new shoes,
prettily stitched and polished to perfection.

"Impossible," he thought, rubbing his eyes.
But there were the shoes, gleaming in the
sunlight. "Look at this," he called to his wife.
"Someone finished my shoes last night!"

"Whoever it was, they've done a wonderful job," she exclaimed.

They sold the shoes for a gold coin, and used the money to buy more leather.

"Enough for two pairs," the shoemaker told his wife happily, reaching for his scissors. *Snip, snip, snippety-snip.* By the end of the day, he had cut out the pieces for two tall pairs of boots.

"I'll finish them tomorrow," he said.

But in the morning, there stood two pairs of beautiful new boots, neatly stitched, with bright brass buckles, which he sold for four gold coins...

And so it went on. Each day, the shoemaker bought more leather and cut it out, and each night, someone else stitched it into the most magnificent boots and shoes.

Now the shoemaker's shop was filled with customers, and money poured in. But he still had no idea who was helping him. So one night, he and his wife hid behind a curtain to watch...

They had almost dozed off when the door creaked open. Two ragged little men tiptoed over the threshold. "Elves," breathed the shoemaker, his eyes wide with surprise.

The elves climbed quietly onto the table. Their tiny fingers flashed and flew, until they had stitched and polished a whole row of shiny new shoes and boots. And then they left.

"Poor things," sighed the shoemaker. "Working so hard to help us, when they have nothing but rags themselves."

"Let's make them some new clothes in return," suggested his wife.

The shoemaker nodded.

That day, instead of cutting leather as usual, he made two tiny pairs of elf boots, while his wife sewed two tiny elf suits. At bedtime, they laid their gifts on the table, then hid in the corner and waited...

In the middle of the night, the door creaked again. There was a pitter-patter of tiny footsteps and a squeal of delight. "Look, new clothes!"

The elves put them on at once. When they caught sight of themselves in the mirror, they turned cartwheels for sheer joy. They skipped all around the room, singing:

We look so smart, in our new suits,
Too smart by far, for stitching boots!

Then they danced out of the door, still singing.

The old shoemaker and his wife looked at each other and smiled. They didn't mind losing their magic helpers. Now they had plenty of money and customers, and lots of ideas for new shoes. They were back in business – thanks to the elves.

Aladdin and the Magic Lamp

Aladdin was a poor boy, with
no family except his mother.
Or so he thought until, one day,
a man wearing magician's robes
stopped him in the street...

"Aladdin! It's me, Ebenezer."

"Eb-eh-who?" stuttered Aladdin.

The man flashed a toothy smile. "I'm your long-lost uncle. Do as I say and you will make your fortune."

"Well, I could use some money," Aladdin thought. So he followed the man to a lonely mountainside, and watched him mutter some magic words. The ground split open with a noise like thunder. Aladdin shivered.

"Down there is a cave full of treasure," said Ebenezer, pointing. "Take what you like – just bring me the old oil lamp you will find. Hurry!"

Aladdin took a deep breath and climbed down. Slowly his eyes adjusted to the gloom...

He gasped. Before him was a cavern filled with glittering fruit trees. On each tree grew gems of astonishing size and beauty, and on the ground between them lay a battered old brass lamp.

Aladdin crammed his pockets with great bunches of rubies, emeralds and diamonds. Under one tree, he found a carved brass ring, which he slipped onto his finger. Then he picked up the lamp and made his way back.

"Pass me the lamp," said Ebenezer, reaching down greedily.

Something in his face made Aladdin wary. "Help me up first," he insisted.

"The lamp!" snarled Ebenezer.

Aladdin shook his head.

"Then stay there and rot!" Ebenezer yelled.

He stamped his foot and the ground closed again, leaving Aladdin alone in the dark.

"What shall I do now?" he wondered. "Um. Maybe I can light this lamp..." He rubbed it on his sleeve. *Kazoom!* A huge, smoky figure appeared. "A genie!" cried Aladdin.

"I am the Genie of the Lamp," boomed the figure. "Your wish is my command."

"Please, take me home," begged Aladdin.

The genie snapped his fingers. Suddenly, Aladdin was outside his mother's house.

"Where did you come from?" she exclaimed. So Aladdin explained... "That magician was a liar," she said, when he had finished. "You don't have an uncle. But he was right about a fortune – look at those gems!"

"The real treasure is the lamp," said Aladdin. "No wonder he wanted it so badly."

Now Aladdin and his mother were no
longer poor. Whatever they wished for, the
Genie of the Lamp would bring. And so they
lived happily – until Aladdin met the
Sultan's daughter, beautiful Princess
Badra, and they fell hopelessly in love.
Aladdin pined and sighed, until his
mother knew she had to do something.

"Let's offer your gems to the Sultan
and ask for Badra's hand in marriage," she said.

The Sultan was very impressed with
the gems. He was less impressed to discover
Aladdin was just an ordinary boy. "How can you
keep my daughter in a manner
fit for a princess?" he boomed.

"Easy," replied
Aladdin, reaching for
the lamp.

Kazoom! The genie floated before him. "I need a magnificent golden palace..."

The genie snapped his fingers.

Amazed, the Sultan agreed to the wedding at once. Aladdin and Badra were thrilled.

The celebrations lasted for days and people came from far and wide to see them. Among the crowds was the wicked magician Ebenezer. "That wretched boy must be using the lamp," he muttered. "But it won't last. I'll see to that."

He waited until Aladdin had gone out one day, then took a tray of lamps and stood by the palace. "New lamps for old!" he called.

Princess Badra leaned out of a window. "Here's an old one," she said, holding up a battered brass lamp. She didn't know about the genie, so she thought it was a good bargain.

Ebenezer snatched it out of her fingers and rubbed... *Kazoom!* The genie appeared. "Take me and this palace far away!" shouted Ebenezer.

When Aladdin came home, he found only a patch of flattened earth. "Badra!" he cried. He wrung his hands in despair – and accidentally rubbed the carved brass ring he still wore.

Kazam! A wispy figure hovered before him. "I am the Genie of the Ring."

"Please, bring back my wife," begged Aladdin.

"I can't," said the genie. "My magic isn't as strong as that of the lamp. But I can take you to her."

The genie snapped his fingers, and Aladdin was in the stolen palace. As soon as he and Badra had finished hugging, they began to plan their escape...

That evening, Badra offered Ebenezer a drink. He swallowed it in two gulps and fell fast asleep, for it was laced with sleeping potion. Then Badra took the lamp from his pocket and tiptoed out, to where Aladdin was waiting.

Aladdin rubbed his ring. *Kazam!* "Carry Ebenezer to the cave under the mountain," he told the genie, "and lock him up!"

Badra rubbed the lamp. *Kazoom!* "Now, please take us home," she said.

With a smile, the genie did. And this time, without a wicked magician to spoil things, they lived happily ever after.

The Three Wishes

One fine day, an old man was
out gathering mushrooms.
He was about to pick an extra large
one when he heard a tiny voice
shout, "Please stop!"

The old man looked down – and blinked. There, peering out of the mushroom, was a fairy! She had made her home inside it.

"If you spare my mushroom, I will give you three wishes," she said.

The old man didn't think twice. "Thank you!" he cried, and hurried off to share the good news with his wife. "What should we wish for first?" he wondered. "A grand house, fancy clothes, a sack full of gold...?"

"You're early," said his wife, when she saw him. "Supper isn't ready yet."

"Oh," sighed the old man, feeling his tummy rumble. "I wish I had a nice sausage."

Ting! A fat, juicy sausage appeared on the table. His wife stared. "How did you do that?" So the old man explained...

"You silly man," cried his wife. "Wasting a wish on a sausage. I wish your sausage was on the end of your nose!"

Ting! The sausage dangled from the old man's nose.

"Oh no, I didn't mean it." She tried to pull the sausage off, but it wouldn't budge.

"Ow!"

"I'm sorry. Well, we still have one wish left. What will it be?"

The old man patted his sausage-nose gingerly. "I can't stay like this."

His wife nodded. "I wish that sausage was back on the table," she said. *Ting!* It was. "So much for our three wishes," she sighed. "But at least we'll have sausage for supper!"

Edited by Lesley Sims

Designed by Caroline Spatz

First published in 2013 by Usborne Publishing Ltd., Usborne House, 83-85 Saffron Hill, London EC1N 8RT, England. www.usborne.com
Copyright © 2013 Usborne Publishing Ltd.

Usborne
Royal
Fairy Tales
for
Bedtime

Retold by Mairi Mackinnon

Illustrated by Lorena Alvarez

Contents

5

The Princess and the Pea

based on a story by Hans Christian Andersen

13

The Frog Prince

based on a story by the Brothers Grimm

21

The Emperor's New Clothes

based on a story by Hans Christian Andersen

29

The Twelve Dancing Princesses

based on a story by the Brothers Grimm

39

Sleeping Beauty

based on a story by Charles Perrault

47

The Emperor and the Nightingale

based on a story by Hans Christian Andersen

57

The Firebird

based on a Russian folk tale

65

The Snow Queen

based on a story by Hans Christian Andersen

85

The Flying Horse

based on a story from the *Arabian Nights*

The Princess and the Pea

O nce upon a time, there was a
prince who wanted to marry
a princess. "And she must be a
real princess," he insisted.

"Of course she must," agreed his parents, the King and Queen. "We'll send for the royal heralds and announce it at once."

"I think I'd rather find her for myself," said the prince. So he summoned his servants, who packed his bags and saddled the horses, and together they all set out.

The prince went from city to city and from country to country, meeting all kinds of princesses. Some of them were dazzlingly beautiful. Some were rich and grand, and lived in magnificent palaces. Some were clever, some were gentle and kind. The prince was impressed and he was charmed, but he was never quite sure that any one of them was a *real* princess.

The prince and his servants rode on, further and further from home, to chilly mountain castles and to crumbling desert forts. They found princesses who sang sweetly or danced beautifully, and the prince admired their performances and clapped politely at the end. Some princesses made him laugh, and a few even made him cry. Still, each time he had a nagging doubt: was *this* one a real princess?

"Your Highness, how will you tell?" asked his servants.

The prince sighed. "I can't explain it," he said. "But when I meet one, I'm sure I'll know."

At last, even the prince had to admit that the search was hopeless. Wearily, he made his way home again, and his parents didn't know how to cheer him up.

One evening soon after, there was a terrible storm. Lightning flashed and the rain lashed down, and in the middle of it all there was a knock at the palace door. There stood a girl all drenched and draggled, who said she was a lost princess. A *real* princess.

"With no coach and no servants?" thought the King.

"With no fine gown and jewels?" thought the Queen; but they invited her in all the same, and gave orders for a hot bath and towels and a change of clothes to be laid out for her.

Once she was dry and dressed again, the girl did look a little more like a princess. They all sat down to supper together and the prince thought she was quite charming. The King and Queen smiled to themselves: the prince hadn't looked so happy in weeks.

"My dear, you must stay the night," said the Queen. She ordered a bed to be made up, and went upstairs herself to make sure that everything was done exactly as she wanted.

First, she placed a pea in the middle of the bed. Then she had twenty mattresses piled on top of it, with twenty quilts on top of that. Finally, she had a ladder brought in so that the poor girl could get in and out of bed. It looked a little strange, but nobody said a word.

In the morning, the princess came downstairs looking pale and tired.

"How did you sleep, my dear?" asked the Queen.

"Oh!" said the princess, looking embarrassed. "You've been very kind... but I was so uncomfortable! I could feel a lump somewhere under the mattresses. I've hardly slept at all."

The Queen smiled, and the prince's face lit up. "So sensitive!" he exclaimed. "You *must* be a real princess."

And so they were married, and the pea was placed in a glass case in the Palace museum. Who knows, it may still be there today.

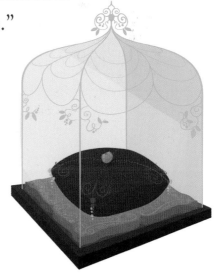

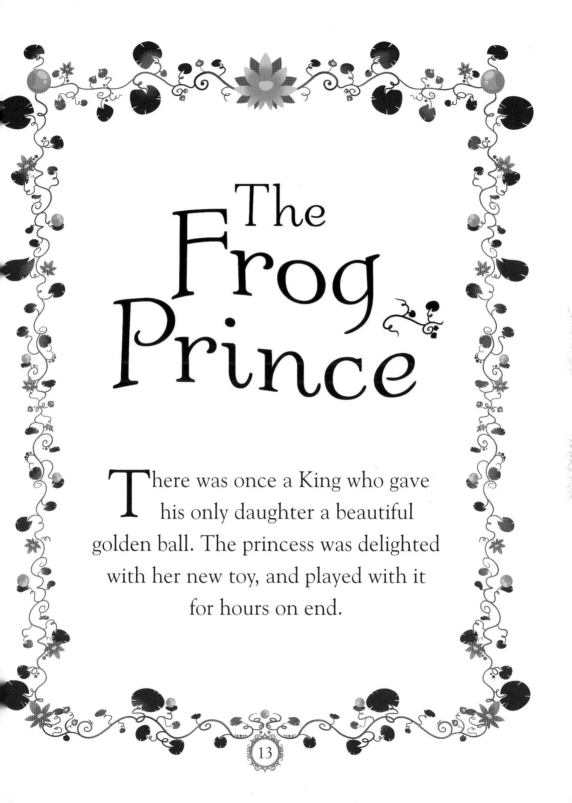

The Frog Prince

There was once a King who gave his only daughter a beautiful golden ball. The princess was delighted with her new toy, and played with it for hours on end.

On hot summer days, she liked going out to the palace gardens, where there were shady trees beside a deep, cool well. One sunny afternoon, she was playing there, tossing her ball high in the air and catching it again. Suddenly it slipped through her fingers, splashed into the murky well water and vanished.

The princess was horrified. "My ball!" she wailed. "Papa's present! How will I ever get it back?" She peered into the well, but the walls were so steep and the water looked so deep, she didn't dare climb in.

"Don't cry," croaked a little voice. "Let me help you."

The princess looked around, but all she could see was a shiny green frog, perched on the well's edge.

"What will you do for me if I find your ball for you?" asked the frog.

"Oh, anything," sobbed the princess. "I'll give you gold, jewels, whatever you want..."

"Gold and jewels are no use to me," said the frog. "Will you be my friend? Will you let me eat with you and drink with you, and sleep on your pillow at night?"

"Yes, yes, I promise, anything," sniffed the princess. "But what's the use? You can't bring my ball back, can you?"

The frog dived into the water, and jumped right out again with the ball clutched between his webbed front feet.

Amazed, the princess snatched it up and ran to the palace. Faintly behind her she could hear a croaking:

"Wait, Princess! I can't keep up with you! Princess! You... pro... mised!"

She ran even faster, not daring to look back. When she reached the door of the palace, she slipped inside and bolted the door behind her.

That evening, the princess was sitting down to supper with the King and Queen when they heard a faint *splash, splosh* outside the hall.

Everyone fell quiet. Then a voice croaked, "Princess! You promised!"

The princess gasped and dropped her soup spoon. She reddened as everyone stared at her.

The King turned to his daughter. "What's this?" he asked. She burst into tears and told her parents everything.

"If you made a promise, then you must keep it," the King said sternly.

The door swung open and the frog hopped into the room. Nobody said a word as he hopped across the floor and then up onto the table beside the princess. She watched in horror as he sipped from her soup bowl. "Delicious!" he said.

The princess made a face and pushed the bowl away. She ran from the table, out of the hall and up to her room, but the frog was right behind her, *splash, splosh, splash, splosh...*

"You're NOT sleeping on my pillow!" the princess shouted. She picked up the frog, screwed her eyes shut and hurled him as hard as she could across the room.

Immediately, she felt ashamed. "Oh, Frog, I shouldn't have done that. I'm so sorry!" she murmured, and opened her eyes.

To her astonishment, there was no sign of the frog. Instead, there stood a kind-looking prince. "Thank you!" he cried. "A wicked witch cast a spell on me. She said it could only be broken if anyone ever felt sorry for me – and who would feel sorry for a slimy old frog? But you've set me free at last."

"Have I really?" gasped the princess.

"So now do you think we can be friends?" he asked.

"Of course!" smiled the princess. "Are you hungry? Shall we go back down to supper?"

The Emperor's New Clothes

Once upon a time, there was a
rich and powerful Emperor.
He ruled over mountains, forests
and lakes, and over towns,
villages and islands.

He wasn't in the least
interested in his empire,
though, or his palaces and
treasures. All he cared
about was clothes. He had
magnificent outfits for
morning, noon and
night, every day of the
week. He spent hours dressing
up to go out, then going out to be admired.

When he inspected his armies, he would
ask how *they* thought *he* looked. When he went
to the opera or the ballet, he was sure to be
more spectacular than anything on the stage.
Even so, whenever he put on a new outfit, he
was soon tired of it. "It looks so... ordinary," he
would complain. "Surely I can do better. I am
the Emperor, after all."

One day, two strangers came to the palace gates and made an announcement. "We are weavers of the finest cloth," they said, "and makers of the finest suits. Our cloth is really rather special. You see, only people who are truly intelligent or good at their jobs can see it."

"What a brilliant idea!" thought the Emperor. "With a suit like that, I could soon tell which of my ministers isn't fit to serve me. Only the good ones will be able to see that I'm wearing it. I must order one at once."

The two men were shown into the throne room, where they bowed deeply and murmured, "Your Majesty! We are so flattered! Truly, we don't deserve... Of course, we would be delighted to make a suit for you!"

The men lost no time in setting up their loom at the palace, and asking for bags and bags of gold in payment. They bought reel after reel of bright silks and precious gilt threads, but it was all packed away out of sight. Then they made themselves busy, their shuttles flying to and fro through the empty air.

The Emperor waited impatiently, and after a little while he thought, "I must find out how my suit is coming along." But then a terrible doubt struck him. "What if I can't see the cloth? What if *I* am no good at my job?"

"I'll ask the Prime Minister," he decided. "He's a clever man, he's sure to see it."

So the Prime Minister went to visit the weavers. He was shocked by the empty loom, but he didn't dare admit that he couldn't see any cloth. Instead, he told the Emperor, "Your Majesty, it really is a wonder. So fine! So rich! Such an exquisite pattern!"

At last, the men decided that the cloth should be ready. They took it off the loom, then cut the air with giant scissors. They pinned and they stitched, then proudly brought their work to the Emperor.

"I can't see anything!" thought the Emperor in a panic.

"We can't see anything!" thought all his courtiers; but no one dared to say so out loud.

The Emperor let the men dress him, pulling and patting the invisible cloth. His courtiers pretended to pick up his long cloak, and they all set out to parade through the town.

Everyone had heard about the amazing suit, and crowds lined the streets. They gazed in silence, ashamed to think that they were too stupid to see the wonderful fabric.

Then suddenly a little boy cried: "Daddy! The Emperor isn't wearing any clothes!" Soon the whole crowd was murmuring, "It's true! The Emperor has no clothes!"

There was a sudden gust of wind. The Emperor shivered, but what could he do? He walked bravely on with his head held high.

No one saw the two weavers, shaking with laughter as they scurried away. The crooks crept through the town gate and were never seen again.

The Twelve Dancing Princesses

There was once a King who had twelve beautiful daughters. They slept in twelve beds, all together in one big room at the top of a tower.

Every night the door to their tower was shut, locked and guarded, but every morning the princesses came down to breakfast pale and tired, and their maids found their dancing shoes all worn out.

The princesses wouldn't say where they'd been, and no one else could explain it.

"I won't have secrets in *my* palace," stormed the King. "If you won't tell me, I'll find someone who can. The man who solves the mystery in three nights may marry whichever princess he chooses, and inherit my kingdom after I die."

Soon there were princes and lords lining up to try their luck. The princesses made them all very welcome, and each one was shown to a small room next to the princesses' bedroom. Somehow, though, they never could stay awake through the night...

...and if they failed in their task three nights running, the King had them banished from the land.

One day, a soldier came trudging through the country, home from the wars, and fell into conversation with an old woman on the road.

"That's a strange story about the princesses," he said. "I thought I might try and find the answer myself."

The old woman laughed. "Why not? Just remember, don't drink anything the princesses give you, and pretend to fall fast asleep. Oh, and you may find this useful." She handed him a long, dark cloak. "Wear it, and you can follow the princesses without being seen. Good luck!"

That night, the princesses smiled sweetly at the soldier, and offered him a warm drink. "We made it ourselves," they said. "It's delicious." The soldier thanked them, but he poured it out of a window when they weren't looking. Then he climbed into bed and pretended to snore loudly.

A little while later, he heard the princesses' excited chatter next door. He slipped on his cloak, and tiptoed into their room.

The girls were dressed in shimmering ballgowns, their faces bright. They had pushed one of the beds aside and opened a trapdoor underneath it. The soldier was just in time to follow them down a winding staircase.

At the bottom of the stairs stood a forest of tall trees, with silver leaves that gleamed in the moonlight. The soldier broke off a silvery twig, and the youngest princess whirled around. "What's that noise? Someone's following us!"

"Don't be frightened, little one," said her sisters. "No one's ever found the way before. That old soldier would sleep through forty fanfares. It's probably just a fox in the bushes."

After the silver forest, they came to a golden one, and then another with leaves of diamonds. Each time, the soldier took another twig and hid it under his cloak. The youngest princess looked around anxiously, but she didn't say anything to her sisters.

They reached a glassy lake, where twelve princes were waiting in lantern-lit boats to row the princesses across. The soldier stepped into the last boat, along with the youngest princess.

"How strange!" said the prince. "I'm rowing as hard as ever, but we're far behind the others. And look how low our boat is in the water!"

On the other side was a castle, with bright lights and music spilling from all the doors and windows. The princes and princesses went in and joined the dancing, and the soldier went with them, skipping invisibly between the couples. Finally, as the sun rose, the princes rowed the sleepy princesses back across the lake.

When they landed, the soldier raced ahead, through the forests and up the stairs. By the time the princesses came in, he was safely in his bed, and they laughed to hear his snores.

For two more nights, the soldier followed the princesses. Sometimes he danced in among them, sometimes he helped himself from the feast laid out between dances: an almond cake here, a handful of grapes there. On the last night, he even slipped a golden goblet under his cloak. Sometimes he snoozed in a corner, but he was always ready to follow the princesses when the princes rowed them back across the lake.

On the third morning, the King summoned him and said, "So, where do my daughters go at night?"

The princesses giggled, then gasped as the soldier produced a velvet bag and took out the precious twigs and the goblet.

"They go through a secret trapdoor to an underground kingdom," he said, "to a castle by a lake. Twelve princes ferry them across the lake to the castle. They dance there all night, and then the princes bring them back at first light."

The King could see from his daughters' shocked faces that the soldier was telling the truth. "You shall have your reward," he said. "Which princess do you choose?"

"Well," said the soldier, "I'm not so young any more. I'd be happy to marry the eldest, if she'll have me."

They were married that same afternoon, and the whole country celebrated their wedding. The dancing went on for a week.

Sleeping Beauty

Once upon a time, there was a King and a Queen who desperately wanted to have children. When at last the Queen had a baby daughter, there were celebrations all through the land.

"We must have a feast for her christening," said the King, and he invited seven fairies to be the baby's godmothers. Each fairy gave the little princess a special gift. "She will be as beautiful as a rose," said the first. "Graceful as a lily," said the second; and the others promised in turn that she would be sweet-natured and talented, she would sing like a nightingale, and dance...

Suddenly, the castle doors burst open and a furious fairy stormed in. She was dressed in a tattered black gown, and her face was creased with spite. Shocked, the guests drew back as she strode through the hall.

"Haven't you forgotten someone?" she sneered.

"Carabos!" whispered the Queen. "We didn't think..."

Glowering over the baby's cradle, the fairy Carabos raised her wand. "*This* is my gift to you," she said. "When you are sixteen years old, you will prick your finger on a spindle and die!"

The guests gasped, and the Queen fainted. Then the seventh fairy stepped forward. "I haven't given my gift yet," she said. "I can't undo this wicked curse, but perhaps I can make it a little better. The princess won't die, but she will fall asleep for a hundred years."

The next day, the King passed a law to ban spinning wool with spindles, and he gave orders for every spindle in the land to be destroyed. Bonfires were built on every town square and village green, and for sixteen years, there wasn't a spindle to be found anywhere.

On her sixteenth birthday, the princess was happily playing hide-and-seek with her friends when she found the door to a distant tower.

"I've never seen that before," she thought. Curiously, she climbed the steep stair. At the top was a tiny round room, and an old lady sitting by the window with a handful of wool and a strange, whirling, wooden thing.

"Oh! What are you doing?" asked the princess.

"Spinning, my dear," said the old lady. "Look, I'm making thread. Would you like to try?

But as soon as the princess touched the spindle, she cried out and fell to the ground. The old lady called for help and servants came rushing in, but nobody could wake the princess.

They carried her to her bedroom and laid
her down on her bed. As soon as her head
touched the pillow, everyone in the castle sank
into a deep sleep. The King and Queen nodded
off on their thrones, and the lords and ladies
slumped on their velvet stools. The cooks in the
kitchens, the maids and the footmen, the guards
on the battlements, all lay down and slept. Even
the horses nodded off in the stables, the dogs
drowsed in the yard and the swallows
fell silent in the eaves.

A hundred years passed, and
a tangle of wild roses grew up
around the castle until only the
tops of the towers could be seen.
The King, the Queen and the
princess were all forgotten,
and a new king ruled the land.

One day, a prince was riding by, and noticed the turrets above the thorny branches. He couldn't help wondering what lay inside. Jumping down from his horse, he took his sword and started hacking through the wild rose stems.

He reached the castle, and was shocked to see still figures everywhere. "Are they dead?" he wondered; but he quickly realized that they were only sleeping. He wandered from room to room until he came to the princess's bedroom. She was so beautiful that he couldn't resist kissing her.

The princess smiled and opened her eyes.

"Will you marry me?" breathed the prince.

"Oh, *yes*," she said.

The birds started singing and the dogs barked. Hand in hand, the prince and princess hurried downstairs to tell her parents their good news... and slowly the castle came back to life.

The Emperor and the Nightingale

L ong ago, the Emperor of China
lived in a magnificent palace.
It was surrounded by gardens full of
beautiful flowers, and silver bells
that tinkled in the breeze.

Beyond the gardens was a forest of tall trees and still, quiet lakes. Beyond the forest was the sea, and right next to the sea lived a nightingale.

The nightingale was a plain-looking little bird, but she sang so beautifully that everyone who heard her stopped to listen and sigh and smile. People came from far and wide to visit the Emperor's palace. They wrote long, learned books about all the wonders they had seen, but they all agreed that the nightingale's song was the greatest wonder of all.

In time, the Emperor happened to read one of these books. He frowned. "What is this nightingale?" he said. "If it's so special, why don't I know about it?"

He called for his ministers, but none of them had heard of the nightingale. "Bring it to me!" the Emperor ordered. "By tonight!"

The ministers and the palace servants were all in a panic. If the Emperor didn't get what he wanted, they knew they would be punished, but no one even knew what a nightingale was or where to start looking for one. Finally, a kitchen girl spoke up.

"I know the nightingale. When I go to visit my mother by the seashore, I sometimes hear her singing. It's the sweetest music you ever heard."

"Quickly, show us the way!" said the ministers, and they followed the girl out of the palace.

In the fields, they heard a cow mooing. "Is that the nightingale?" they asked eagerly.

"No, no," she laughed. "Wait a while."

By the lake, they heard frogs croaking. "The nightingale, surely!"

"Not yet," she smiled.

They reached the seashore just as the light was fading. "Hush!" said the girl, and the nightingale began to sing.

"Beautiful," breathed the ministers. When the music finished, the grandest of them, the Lord Chamberlain, cleared his throat. "Little bird, the Emperor would be pleased to hear your song. We have come to bring you to the palace."

"My song sounds best here in the open air," said the nightingale, "but if the Emperor has asked for me, I will come."

That evening, the whole court gathered to listen to the nightingale. As she started to sing, the crowds fell still. Silvery notes filled the air, and the Emperor listened with tears in his eyes.

The nightingale's song ended, and the Emperor started clapping loudly. "Bravo! Bravo indeed! Little bird, how can I reward you?"

"There's no need," she said simply. "An Emperor's tears are better than any reward."

From that day, the nightingale was the most important guest in the palace. She had a golden cage, and was allowed to fly out three times a day, with twelve servants holding ribbons tied to her leg. (She didn't enjoy this much, but she was too polite to say so.)

Everyone in the palace and across the whole country talked about the nightingale. Some even tried to imitate her singing, although of course they sounded nothing like her.

One day, a messenger arrived with a gift for the Emperor. "From your friend, the Emperor of Japan," he explained.

Inside the box was a clockwork bird, covered with jewels and with a large golden key. "Another nightingale!" exclaimed the Emperor. He turned the key. "Let's hear them together."

The real nightingale tried to sing along with the golden toy, but she couldn't match its stiff rhythms and mechanical phrases. "The new nightingale is better!" said the courtiers as the Emperor wound it again. "It's prettier! And you know exactly what it is going to sing!" Nobody noticed the real nightingale, quietly flying away.

Soon the toy nightingale was even more popular than the real one. It sang day and night, and its song was easy to learn. Then one day, instead of singing, it made a terrible whirring sound.

The Emperor sent for the royal watchmaker, who opened up the bird and poked and prodded inside. "The mechanism is too fragile," he said. "I will fix it as well as I can, but you won't be able to play it more than once a year."

The Emperor was horribly disappointed. He missed his nightingale badly, and soon became pale and ill. Servants tiptoed through the palace, and ministers began to talk quite openly about who should be the next Emperor. It was as if he had died already.

The Emperor lay in his great carved bed, and in the shadowy corners he seemed to see ghosts, muttering about all the good and bad things he had done in his life. "Hush! I can't bear it!" he cried. He tried to wind up his toy bird, but he was too weak. His eyes filled with tears.

Then a pure silver sound filled the room. The Emperor opened his eyes to see the real nightingale on his windowsill. The ghosts had vanished.

"Dear nightingale," he said. "I've missed you so much. Please come back to stay."

"I can't live in a palace," said the nightingale, "but I can visit you and I always will. My friend Emperor, your ministers are coming. How glad they will be to find you alive and well."

The Firebird

There was once a prince named Ivan who loved riding through the forest with his horse and hounds. One morning, he caught sight of a dazzlingly bright bird through the trees.

Its long wings and tail feathers glowed like fire, bright among the branches. Prince Ivan wheeled his horse around and galloped after it, but however fast he rode, he couldn't catch up.

Further and further he rode. Towards evening he glimpsed the bird again, flying into the gardens of a palace that he had never seen before. Stepping down from his horse, Prince Ivan opened the gate to a magical orchard. All around him were trees bearing golden apples, and eerie stone statues of knights.

Suddenly he saw a halo of light. Tiptoeing

closer, he caught the beautiful bird in his arms.

"Have mercy!" begged the Firebird. "Don't kill me!"

"Kill you?" echoed the prince. "Of course not!"

"Let me go free," she said, "and I will give you this feather. If you should ever need me, I will fly back to help you." Spreading her wings, she soared into the sky.

Left alone, Prince Ivan realized how late it was, and how far he was from home. Just then, he heard the sound of voices. Chattering and laughing, twelve beautiful girls came into the garden, followed by a princess who was lovelier still. They plucked the golden apples from the trees, playing catch with them in the moonlight.

Prince Ivan watched them for a while, then stepped out of the shadows and smiled. "Don't be afraid," he said. "May I join your game?"

By dawn, Ivan had fallen deeply in love with the princess. As the sky grew lighter, though, the girls looked anxious. "We must go back to the palace," the princess said, "and you should leave. It isn't safe for you here."

"Why not?" asked Ivan.

"The palace belongs to the ogre Koshchey," explained the princess. "He is a powerful magician, and we are his prisoners. If he finds you, he will turn you to stone, just like the others."

The prince looked at the statues around the garden and shuddered. "They were once alive?" he whispered. Yet he couldn't bring himself to leave the princess in the ogre's power. He marched up to the palace and wrenched open its great iron doors.

A peal of jangling bells rang out, and a hundred hideous demons spilled into the garden, followed by the ogre himself. Koshchey was furious to see Prince Ivan. He was raising his arms to cast a spell when Ivan remembered the Firebird's feather.

"Help me, please," he murmured.

Light filled the garden as the Firebird swooped down. Fluttering from tree to tree, she led Koshchey and the demons on a crazy dance until they slumped to the ground, exhausted.

"Quickly! Look in the hollow tree," the Firebird called to Ivan, pointing with her long beak. Ivan reached into the hollow and pulled out an iron-bound box. Inside was a gleaming golden egg.

"Take it," whispered the Firebird. "It's Koshchey's soul. Destroy it, and you destroy Koshchey and all his creatures."

The prince cradled the egg in his hands. The ogre jerked awake, screaming when he saw what Ivan had found. Ivan squeezed the egg, and Koshchey doubled up. Ivan tossed it from one hand to the other, and Koshchey flew helplessly through the air.

Finally, Ivan held the egg high and hurled it to the ground. The ogre, the demons and the orchard all vanished in a clap of thunder. All that remained were the statues. As the sun rose, their faces flushed with life and they stretched stiffly, muttering their surprise.

The princess rushed into Ivan's arms, and together they watched the Firebird, soaring away into the heart of the sun.

The Snow Queen

🌸 Part I 🌸

Long ago, two children lived in a crowded city, high up in two tall houses that were almost touching. Their names were Kay and Gerda, and they were best friends.

In the summer, they grew red and white roses in their windowboxes, and chatted to each other through the open windows. In the winter, they stayed inside where it was warm, and listened to Gerda's grandmother telling stories.

One December evening, while the snow whirled outside, Grandmother said, "Stay safely here, my dears, and keep away from the Snow Queen. She'll be out there, somewhere, in the thickest part of the storm."

Kay pressed his face to the window, and saw a lady's beautiful white-cold face. She wore  an icy crown, and her eyes glittered like midwinter stars. She waved to Kay and smiled, but he was afraid to look at her and he turned away.

As he turned, he felt a sharp pain in his eye, and another in his heart. The Snow Queen had planted splinters of ice there so that he could no longer see or feel the goodness in anything.

"Grandmother, I don't understand it," said Gerda, a few days later. "Why is Kay so angry and mean? He makes me cry, but he just laughs."

Kay didn't want to play with Gerda any more. "Growing flowers is for girls," he sneered. "Stories are for babies." Instead, he liked going to play with the big boys in the snowy cathedral square.

One afternoon, he saw a splendid silvery sleigh with a driver all wrapped in furs. "Don't you recognize me?" said the Snow Queen. "Come and sit beside me."

Kay thought she was the most beautiful person he had ever seen. She bent to kiss his forehead with icy cold lips. Then they set off, and the snow flurried around them as they swept out of the city gate. Faster and faster, they flew through the air to the Snow Queen's palace.

Kay was gone, and nobody knew what had happened to him. "He often went tobogganing down by the river," said the boys in the square. "Maybe he fell through the ice and drowned." No one except Gerda seemed to care.

In the spring, she went down to the river. "Please bring my friend back," she whispered. "I'll give you my new red shoes." She threw her shoes into the water, but the river just washed them back again. "Maybe I didn't throw them far enough," Gerda thought. Stepping into a boat, she pushed off from the river bank.

The boat began drifting down the river, catching the current and gathering speed, and Gerda couldn't do anything to stop it. "Perhaps at least it will take me to Kay," she thought.

At last, the boat drifted around a bend and on to the bank. There stood a neat little cottage, with an old lady in a sunhat working in the garden. "Can I help you, my dear?" she called. She held the boat steady as Gerda clambered out. "Sit down and rest, you poor thing."

"Such a pretty little girl," thought the old lady. "If only she could stay here forever..." Gently she combed Gerda's hair, soothing her to sleep, combing the memories away. She even cut down the roses outside her house so that Gerda wouldn't see them and remember her home.

The old lady was kind, and Gerda stayed happily enough, although sometimes she found herself thinking that something was missing. Then, one summer morning, she noticed the old lady's sunhat lying on a chair, with its pattern of...

"Roses!" she realized. "Kay!" she cried. "Oh, what am I doing?"

She ran from the house, stumbling through the woods with tears in her eyes, until she had to stop and rest. A curious crow hopped down beside her. "Little girl, why are you crying?"

"Oh, dear crow, I am looking for my friend Kay. Have you seen him?" Gerda told her story, and the crow hopped excitedly. "Maybe I have, maybe I have," he cawed.

"You see," he continued, "our princess recently decided to get married. She advertised in the newspapers, and all the fine gentlemen came calling, but she didn't care for any of them – until a brown-haired boy came along, with shiny black boots that squeaked."

"That's Kay!" said Gerda. "Those were his new boots; he was so proud of them."

The crow continued: "He told the princess he only wanted to talk to her because he'd heard she was so wise. Of course, that impressed her more than anything, so now he is a prince."

"Lucky Kay," sighed Gerda. "Can we go and see him, do you think?"

"I know a way into the palace," said the crow. "I'll show you."

"We'd better wait until night, though," he added. "If they see you, the guards and the footmen will never let you near the prince and princess in those shabby old clothes." He flew ahead of Gerda to the palace grounds, and went to the kitchens to scavenge some bread for her.

That evening, he showed Gerda to a little door at the foot of a tower, and she followed him up the winding stair. At the top was a magnificent bedroom, with two beds shaped like red and white lilies. In the white lily bed, the princess slept soundly.

Gerda turned to the other bed. She thought her heart might burst. Leaning closer, she whispered, "Kay? Is it you, at last?"

The Snow Queen

❧ Part II ❧

The prince opened his eyes.
"Oh!" sobbed Gerda.
"It isn't Kay at all. It looks
just like him, but it isn't."

The prince sat up sharply and the princess woke in a panic, but when they heard Gerda's story, they were truly sorry for her. The next day, they dressed her in velvet and furs and sent her on her way in a gilded coach.

As night fell, the coach came to a dark forest where a band of robbers noticed its golden glow. They sprang out of the trees, seized the horses and dragged Gerda from the coach.

"She looks tasty!" said an old robber woman, brandishing a cruel knife; but a wild girl with curly black hair jumped up. "No!" she yelled. "I want her to be my friend. She's coming with me in the coach, back to our castle." Gerda was terrified, but she knew the girl meant to be kind.

When they arrived, the girl said, "Come and see my pets." She led Gerda through a high stone hall to a heap of rugs in the corner, where her bed was. Above the bed were a hundred wild pigeons in cages, and next to it was a reindeer tethered to the wall.

"Look at your fancy clothes! Are you a princess?" she asked.

"No," said Gerda, and told her story. "Have you seen him, have you seen Kay?" she asked hopefully.

"We have, we have," cooed the pigeons. "We saw Kay with the Snow Queen in her sleigh, rushing through the air to Lapland. So cold, so cold!"

"To Lapland?" asked Gerda.

"To my country," said the reindeer. "That's where the Snow Queen lives."

"Oh, how can I get there?" cried Gerda.

"You must run away," said the robber girl. "I'll help you. Not now, but tomorrow, when all the men are away. You can take my reindeer, but I think I'll keep your clothes, they're much nicer than mine."

In the morning, she gave Gerda some old clothes of her own, and helped her onto the reindeer's back. "Take care of her, now," she told him, flashing her long knife in warning.

The reindeer sped off through the forest, galloping all day across the snowy plains to Lapland. Just when he was beginning to tire, they saw a distant hut. Gerda tumbled off the reindeer's back, and knocked at the lighted window.

The only person at home was an old woman. "Mercy, however did you get here?" she exclaimed. "Come in and warm yourselves."

When Gerda told her story, the old woman sighed. "Yes, the Snow Queen lives near here, and she has your friend Kay. She's planted ice splinters in his eye and in his heart, too. Oh, he thinks he is happy enough, but he'll never be his old self until he gets rid of those splinters."

"You're very wise," said the reindeer. "Can't you give Gerda some special power to help her?"

"She doesn't need it," the old woman replied. "For a little girl on her own, to have come this far – she is stronger than she knows. Take her to the Snow Queen's palace, and you'll see."

It was only a few miles further to the Snow Queen's palace, but the snow fell thickly and the snowflakes grew bigger, making the shapes of snarling wolves and bears. Terrified, Gerda breathed a prayer – and her breath turned into angel-shapes, marching all around her. The angels beat the snow-creatures away until she could walk freely through the great icy gates.

Inside, she wandered through a hundred snow-filled halls, vast and silent, eerily lit by the Northern Lights. In the biggest hall of all was a great frozen lake, and in the middle of the lake stood the Snow Queen's crystal throne.

The throne was empty: the Snow Queen had gone to whip up blizzards and make mischief in the countries far to the south. Gerda's face fell; and then beside the throne, she saw a figure, white with cold and hardly moving.

"Kay!" cried Gerda. She ran to put her arms around him, and her warm tears went straight to his heart, melting away the ice-splinter there.

Kay looked up, amazed. "Gerda?" he whispered. "You've come all this way to find me?" Tears welled up in his own eyes, washing away the second splinter. The two of them clung to each other, and Kay felt warmth slowly spreading through his body. Then, hand in hand, they walked out of the palace.

The snowstorm had stopped and the sky was clear. On the horizon they could see the bright rising sun, and they followed it southwards.

When they reached the old woman's hut, the snows were starting to melt. In the robber girl's forest there were green buds on the trees, and in the princess's kingdom there were spring flowers in the hedges. Along the river, the apple trees were in blossom, and when they reached the city they saw roses in all the windowboxes.

Gerda's grandmother sat by the open window, dressed in black. When she saw the two children, she could hardly speak for joy. All three held each other close, together again in the warm sun.

The Flying Horse

There was once a king who loved all kinds of magic and mechanical marvels. One day, an inventor presented him with a life-sized ebony horse, patterned with gold.

"Splendid!" said the King. "What can it do?"

"Your Majesty, this horse will fly through the air, faster than the wind," the man declared.

The King's son had been admiring the horse, but now he burst out laughing. "Don't be ridiculous!" he snorted. "How can it possibly fly?"

The inventor glared at him. "See for yourself," he snapped. "Just twist the pin in the right shoulder, and use the reins to steer."

The prince jumped onto the horse's back and twisted the shoulder pin. Everyone gasped as the horse rose high above the palace courtyard.

"How do I get down?" the prince called.

"Ha! You should have thought of that before making fun of me," cackled the inventor.

The prince rose up until he was lost in the clouds. The King raged, the Queen screamed and the inventor was thrown into prison.

Meanwhile, the prince thought: "If there's a pin to make it go up, most likely there's another to come down." Sure enough, he found a pin on the horse's left shoulder, and soon he was swooping down and soaring up through the air.

By evening, he was far from home above a land of green hills and orchards. He saw the domes of a great palace, and came down to land on the roof. Stepping inside, he found a guard dozing by a bedroom door, and in the bedroom was a sleeping princess, so beautiful that he could hardly breathe.

She opened her eyes and smiled shyly. "Who are you?" she asked.

They talked for hours, each finding the other more and more wonderful, until they heard raised voices and the princess's father stormed in. "What thief dares to break into my daughter's bedroom?" he thundered.

"I'm no thief," protested the prince. "I'm a prince who would like to marry your daughter."

"I can't give my daughter to someone who sneaks past my guards," snapped the King. "You deserve to die for your insolence."

The prince thought fast. "Set me a challenge instead," he said. "If I can face your entire army, without a single scratch, then let me marry your daughter."

"Ha!" said the King. "I accept. I have ten thousand soldiers in my army. They'll chop you into ten thousand pieces."

The princess went pale, but the prince smiled to reassure her.

The next morning, the army gathered outside the city gates. It was a terrifying sight, but the prince was calm. "May I at least fight on horseback?" he asked.

"Of course," said the King. "Choose any horse from my stables."

"Thank you," said the prince, "but I'll ride my own horse. You'll find him on the palace roof."

The King's courtiers giggled. When his servants brought the ebony horse, stiff and lifeless, they guffawed. The prince mounted, and the King gave the order to charge.

Slowly, the ebony horse rose into the air.
The prince swooped down here and there and
the soldiers slashed and stabbed, but he was
always out of reach. Then, with a wave, he flew
up to the princess's balcony, helped her into the
saddle and soared away.

By evening, they had reached the prince's
home. As they were landing, the prince saw
black pennants flying and heard loud wailing.

"My darling," he said to the princess.
"Something terrible must have happened. Wait
for me here in the gardens while
I find out what is the matter."
He settled the princess and
hurried into the palace.

As soon as they saw
him, the servants shrieked,
"It's a ghost!"

"Ghost?" said the prince. "Was all that wailing for me? I've never felt more alive."

"We thought the old inventor had killed you! He has been thrown into the dungeons!"

"Well then, you must let him go." And the prince went to find his parents, who were overjoyed to see him.

Meanwhile, the inventor wandered into the gardens, raging at his cruel treatment. With delight, he recognized his ebony horse. When he saw the princess, a plan came into his mind.

"My lady," he said, "the prince has sent me to bring you to the King and Queen. Please, mount your horse and we will go to meet them."

"But I don't know how to ride it," the princess protested.

"Then I will show you," said the inventor, climbing into the saddle after her. He twisted the pin and the horse reared up, but he steered it far away from the palace and over the sea. The princess realized she had been tricked, and she cried bitterly, but the inventor only laughed as they came down to land by a distant forest.

The princess shrieked for help, and out of the forest came a king's hunting party, who soon overpowered the inventor. Bringing them back to his palace, the King made fine apartments ready for the princess, and had the ebony horse placed in his treasure chamber.

The inventor was thrown into prison once again, and it's hard to say who wailed louder, he or the grieving girl.

"Your Majesty, she is ill or she is insane," said his courtiers. "No good will come of this."

"Then send for the best doctors," said the King. "I love her, and she must be cured."

Wise men came with potions and tokens, spells and charms, but they made no difference. One day a young doctor came from a faraway kingdom. "I have some experience in that kind of madness," he said. "Let me see what I can do."

When the princess saw him, she fell quiet for the first time since she had arrived. The King was impressed.

"I'm afraid it won't last," said the mysterious doctor. Sure enough, the princess soon began sobbing again. "I can cure her, but we must go back to the place where you met. Bring everything that you found there."

So they went back to the forest with the princess, the ebony horse and the inventor muttering in his chains.

"There is something about that horse," said the doctor. "Let us mount it, and I will cast a spell to stop its evil power. Now, please, stand back."

Suddenly the inventor recognized the doctor. Too late, he screamed in fury as the prince, princess and horse all soared away.

"I am sorry to deceive you, your Majesty," called the prince. "Truly, I hope that you will find the love you deserve."

He took the princess home to his father's kingdom, and their wedding feast lasted for weeks. The ebony horse became one of the King's greatest treasures, but only after he had destroyed its workings. "It will cause less trouble if it never leaves the ground," he said.

Edited by Lesley Sims
Designed by Russell Punter

Additional design by Laura Wood

First published in 2012 by Usborne Publishing Ltd., Usborne House, 83-85 Saffron Hill,
London EC1N 8RT, England. www.usborne.com
Copyright © 2012 Usborne Publishing Ltd.

USBORNE
ANIMAL STORIES FOR BEDTIME

Retold by Susanna Davidson and Katie Daynes

Illustrated by Richard Johnson

CONTENTS

5

THE TOWN MOUSE AND THE COUNTRY MOUSE

based on one of Aesop's fables

15

THE ELEPHANT'S NOSE

based on a story by Rudyard Kipling

25

THE THREE LITTLE PIGS

based on an English folk tale

33

THE LITTLE RED HEN

based on a Russian folk tale

41

THE BILLY GOATS GRUFF

based on a Norwegian folk tale

51

MOUSE DEER AND THE CROCODILE

based on a Malaysian folk tale

61

CHICKEN LICKEN

based on an English folk tale

69

THE MUSICIANS OF BREMEN

based on a story by The Brothers Grimm

79

THE HARE AND THE TORTOISE

based on one of Aesop's fables

85

THE UGLY DUCKLING,

based on a story by Hans Christian Andersen

THE TOWN MOUSE AND THE COUNTRY MOUSE

A little furry mouse lived in a burrow by a river. His nest was soft with leaves, his cupboards stuffed with berries.

One morning, the little mouse heard a rustling in the undergrowth.

"Surprise!" called a familiar voice. It was his big cousin from the town.

"I thought I'd pay you a visit," the Town Mouse said, "and get some country air."

"How lovely to see you," replied the Country Mouse. "I hope you like it here."

The Town Mouse looked at the towering trees and looming hills. "So, what shall we do?" he asked.

"Let's find some grass to make your bed and gather some nuts for dinner," said the Country Mouse. "Then I'll take you to the waterfall..."

The Town Mouse twitched his whiskers hesitantly. "Lead the way," he said, and scampered after his little cousin.

By sunset he was wet, tired and starving.

"Don't you have anything other than nuts and berries to eat?" he asked.

The Country Mouse offered him some seeds.

"Yuck," spluttered the Town Mouse. He stretched out in his bed. "This grass is too scratchy. I'd prefer newspaper."

The Country Mouse found him some moss.

"I suppose that's *slightly* softer..."

The next day, it just rained and rained and rained. The Country Mouse was happy weaving grass and making berry jelly, but his cousin was bored.

"There's nothing to *do*," he complained. "You must come and stay with me. There's never a dull moment where *I* live."

A shy smile crept beneath the Country Mouse's whiskers. "Why not?" he said.

The next day, they set off through the quiet woods and down a country lane. Gradually, buildings rose up on either side. People tramped up and down and cars roared back and forth.

It was evening before they reached the Town Mouse's home. The sky glowed orange with street lights and the noise from the road was deafening.

"Watch out for the bike!" cried the Town Mouse, as whirling wheels whizzed past them.

"It-it-it nearly hit me!" said the frightened Country Mouse.

"You're fine! Just follow me closely."

He climbed into a pipe, crawled along a stinky tunnel, and came out through a hole into a large, tiled kitchen.

"Dinner time!" announced the Town Mouse.

The Country Mouse let out a squeak of delight. He'd never seen so much food. The table was laden with cakes and the floor was flecked with crumbs.

"Let's eat!" said the Town Mouse, grappling his way up the tablecloth.

His wide-eyed cousin scrambled after him. "I don't know where to start..." he murmured.

He was nibbling on a cake crumb when...

"Cat!" cried the Town Mouse. A large tabby cat had padded silently into the room and was crouching, ready to pounce.

"This way!" the Town Mouse shouted, racing the length of the table and making a daring leap for the mousehole under the kitchen sink.

His little cousin scurried after him, reached the edge of the table and froze.

It was a long way down.

MEOW! went the cat behind him, sending the terrified mouse over the edge. He landed with a bump and tumbled into the mousehole, missing the cat's outstretched claws by a whisker.

"What did I tell you?" said the Town Mouse, cheerfully. "Never a dull moment."

The Country Mouse stared in wonder at his cousin's clean, airy home.

Then he saw a large eye glinting through the entrance hole and a shiver ran down his tail. "How can you ever relax?" he whispered.

"Who wants to relax when there's an adventure around every corner?" replied the Town Mouse. He slid open a matchbox to reveal a golden nugget of cheese. "Here, have a bite."

"Thanks," said the Country Mouse, "but I'm not hungry anymore. I just want to go home."

"To your quiet little burrow?" asked the Town Mouse in surprise.

His cousin nodded. "I think I'd rather have berries and nuts in peace," he said, "than cheese and pie in fear."

The Town Mouse opened his mouth to reply, then shrugged and took a bite of cheese instead.

The next morning, he waved his cousin goodbye. "Come and visit any time!" he cried.

"You too!" replied the Country Mouse.

Do you think they ever did?

THE ELEPHANT'S NOSE

Long, long ago, the elephant had no
trunk – just a little nose, no bigger
than a sausage. She could jiggle it
and wiggle it and waggle it about,
but that was all.

And then along came the Elephant's Child. She was only a little elephant, but she was full of big questions.

"Aunt Ostrich," she said. "Why do your tail feathers grow just so?"

"Uncle Giraffe," she asked. "Why is your skin all spotty?"

"Great Aunt Hippopotamus, why are your eyes so red? Hairy Uncle Baboon, why do melons taste as they do?"

"Run along!" cried her uncles and aunts. "And STOP asking questions."

But the Elephant's Child wanted answers, and she wouldn't be satisfied till she got them.

One day, she asked a new question, one she'd never asked before. "What does a Crocodile have for dinner?"

And everyone said, "Hush!" in quivery, quavery voices.

"But I want to *know*," said the Elephant's Child. "I really do."

"No, you don't," said her uncles and aunts.

And that would have been that, if the Elephant's Child hadn't met the Kolokolo bird, who decided to help her.

"Go all the way to the great, green, greasy Limpopo River," he said. "That's where you'll find your answer."

So the Elephant's Child set out, with a little picnic of red bananas, purple sugarcane and seventeen greeny-juicy melons. She trudged all the way to the Limpopo River, then looked around for a Crocodile. Except, she realized, she had no idea what a Crocodile looked like. She had never seen one before. All she could see was a log.

The log opened one eye, and winked at her. (The log, you see, was actually a Crocodile.)

"Excuse me," said the Elephant's Child, very politely. "Have you seen a Crocodile in these parts?"

The Crocodile winked the other eye and lifted its tail out of the mud. "Come closer, little one. *I* am the Crocodile!"

"Oh!" said the Elephant's Child, coming closer, very breathless and excited. "Will you please tell me what you have for dinner?"

"Come closer, little one," said the Crocodile, "and I will whisper."

The Elephant's Child put her head close to the Crocodile's toothsome mouth and SNAP! The Crocodile caught her by her little nose. "I think," said the Crocodile, between his teeth, "that today, *you* will be my dinner!"

"*Led go!*" cried the Elephant's Child. "*You are hurdig be!*" And she sat back and pulled and pulled as hard as she could. As she did, her nose began to stretch.

The Crocodile floundered in the water, flailing around with his great tail, and *he* pulled and pulled as hard as *he* could.

The Elephant's Child's nose kept on stretching until it was so loooooooong!

She felt her feet slipping in the mud. "*This is too buch for me,*" she said. But at last, the Crocodile let go, landing back in the river with a PLOP that could be heard all the way along the Limpopo.

And SPLAT! The Elephant's Child fell back in the mud, her poor long nose dangling in front of her.

"Ow!" said the Elephant's Child. "It hurts."

So she wrapped her nose
up in cool banana leaves
and waited for it to shrink.
She waited *three* days, but
although it stopped hurting,
it didn't get any smaller.

At the end of the third day, a fly came and
rested on her shoulder and stung her.

Before she knew what she was doing,
the Elephant's Child lifted up her nose and
whacked the fly away.

"I couldn't have done that with my *old* nose,"
thought the Elephant's Child.

Next, she put out her nose, lifted up a
bundle of grass and stuffed it in her mouth. And
when she felt hot, she scooped up a schloop
of mud from the banks of the Limpopo and
slapped it on her head, where it made a cool

sloshy mud cap, all trickly behind her ears.

The Elephant's Child *loved* her new nose. So she went home to show it off.

"What have you done?" cried her family.

"I got a new nose from the Crocodile on the banks of the great, green, greasy Limpopo River," said the Elephant's Child. "I asked him what he had for dinner and he gave me this to keep."

Then all the other elephants set off one by one to get new noses from the Crocodile.

And that is why all the elephants you will ever see, and all the ones you won't, will have noses exactly like the Elephant's Child.

THE THREE LITTLE PIGS

Little pigs don't stay little forever.
There comes a time when
they must find homes
of their own...

"Make sure you build strong, safe houses," warned Mother Pig, as she waved goodbye to her three darling piglets.

"Of course, Mother," replied the first.

"Don't worry," said the second.

"We'll be fine," added the third.

And off they trotted, three not so little pigs, a curl in their tails and not a care in the world.

"Straw for sale!" called a farmer. "Fine and long. Golden yellow. Nature's best."

"Perfect," said the first pig.

He bought three big bundles and made himself a handsome straw hut.

"That was easy," he thought, as he waved goodbye to his brother and sister.

"Build strong, safe houses!" he called after them, putting on their mother's voice.

The two pigs laughed and trotted on into a forest.

"Sticks for sale!" called a woodcutter. "Straight, brown and strong."

"Ah ha," said the second pig. "Sticks are better than straw." She bought three big bundles and made herself a sturdy stick house. Then she waved goodbye to her brother. "Make sure *you* build a strong, safe house," she said, her piggy eyes twinkling.

On trotted the third pig to a factory by a river. A sign above the door said: BRICKS FOR SALE, so he bought three pallets of bricks and a bucket of cement.

It was hard work carrying the heavy bricks and even harder building a brick house, but at last he had a strong, safe home of his own.

Little did the pigs know that a big bad wolf had been following their every move. Prowling the hedgerow, he watched the first pig trot into his handsome straw hut. The wolf licked his lips greedily and strolled up to the door.

"Little pig, little pig, let me in," he growled.

"Not by the hair of my chinny-chin-chin!" replied the pig in a panic.

"Then I'll huff and I'll puff and I'll *blow* your house in."

And he huffed and he puffed, and WHOOSH he blew the house in.

"Help!" squealed the pig, running as fast as his trotters could carry him to his sister's stick house. He only just made it before the wolf was rattling at the door.

"Little pigs, little pigs, let me in," he growled.

"Not by the hairs of our chinny-chin-chins!" replied the petrified pigs.

"Then I'll huff and I'll puff and I'll *blow* your house in."

And he huffed and he puffed...

And he huffed and he puffed...

And CRREEAK he blew the house in.

"Help!" squealed the little pigs, running to their brother's brick house. They felt the wolf's hot breath on their curly tails and quickly shut the door behind them.

"Little pigs, little pigs, let me in!" growled the big bad wolf.

"Not by the hairs of our chinny-chin-chins!"

"Then I'll huff and I'll puff and I'll *blow* your house in."

And he huffed and he puffed...

And he huffed and he puffed...

He huffed and puffed and huffed and puffed... But he just couldn't blow the house in.

"I'm coming to get you!" he yelled suddenly. In one leap he was on the roof. In two leaps he was sliding down the chimney...

He never managed a third leap. He had fallen SPLOSH into a bubbling cooking pot.

The little pigs quickly slammed on the lid, and that was the end of the big bad wolf.

THE LITTLE RED HEN

Once upon a time, in a dusty, cobbled farmyard, a little red hen went peck, peck, peck.

A sleek tabby cat watched her sleepily from a wall, while a proud white goose stood preening her feathers, and a large greedy rat nibbled at a stale crumb.

All of a sudden, the little red hen raised her head. "Grains of wheat!" she clucked excitedly.

"So what?" sniffed the rat. "The farmer scatters them for you every day."

"But we could *plant* them," she announced.

The other animals looked at her as if she were crazy.

"Come on," clucked the hen. "Who's going to help me?"

"Not I," said the rat.

"Not I," said the goose.

"Not I," said the cat.

The hen looked
disappointed.
"Then I shall do
it all by myself,"
she replied. And
she did.

Grain by grain, the hen
carried the wheat in her beak to the edge of
a field. She pecked little holes in the lumpy
brown earth, gently dropped the grains in
and scraped some soil over the top. Then she
walked back to the farmyard.

"Where is your wheat now?" asked the cat,
licking his paws.

"Growing," replied the hen.

And it was. First, bright green shoots popped
their heads out of the soil, then they grew taller,
darker, stronger.

Finally, under the gaze of the summer sun, the wheat plants turned from green to gold.

"It's ready!" cried the hen, fluffing her feathers in delight. "Who will help me to cut it down?"

"Not I," squeaked the rat.

"Not I," honked the goose.

"Not I," purred the cat.

"Then I shall do it all by myself," said the hen. And she did.

The cat, the goose and the rat watched idly from a distance as, one by one, the hen snipped the stalks with her beak. She looked proudly at the pile of golden wheat, then turned to the other animals.

"Now tell me," she clucked, making the cat jump. "Who's going to help me grind this lovely wheat into flour?"

"Not I," huffed the cat.

"Not I," echoed the goose.

"Not I," declared the rat.

"Then I shall do it all by myself," said the hen. And she did.

The others hardly looked up as she walked to and from the mill, carrying as much wheat as her beak could hold. With all her might, she turned the heavy millstone and ground the grains until she had a sack of flour.

"Who will help me make the flour into bread?" she asked, dragging the bag to the farmhouse kitchen.

"Not I," sighed the goose.

"Not I," yawned the cat.

"Not I," groaned the rat.

"Then I shall do that all by myself as well," she puffed.

And she did. She made the flour into a soft, stretchy dough. Before long, wafts of baking bread reached the animals in the farmyard. They rushed to the kitchen window and the goose eagerly tapped her beak on the glass.

The little red hen looked up, amused. "Who will help me eat this bread?" she asked.

"Me!" cried the cat.

"Me!" cried the goose.

"Me!" cried the rat.

"Oh no you won't," said the little red hen, turning back to her warm, crusty loaf. "I had to make this bread all by myself, so I shall eat it *all by myself*."

And she did.

THE BILLY GOATS GRUFF

O nce upon a time there were three Billy Goats, and the name of all three was Gruff.

"I'm hungry," said big Billy Goat Gruff one day.
"Me too," said middle-sized Billy Goat Gruff.
"Me three," said little Billy Goat Gruff.

Big Billy Goat Gruff looked around, at the
bare brown ground. "We need to find more
grass," he announced in his great gruff voice.
"We'll have to cross the Rushing River, to reach
the green fields beyond."

Little Billy Goat Gruff climbed
on some rocks to see. There,
beyond the Rushing River, were
meadows thick with sweet, juicy
grass. He was so excited by the
thought of all that delicious grass
in his tummy, he decided to leave
right away. He jumped down
from the rocks and dashed
along the path to the bridge.

Clippety-clop, clippety-clop went his hooves all along the path, then

TRIP-TRAP, TRIP-TRAP,

TRIP-TRAP

as he trotted across the bridge.

Little Billy Goat Gruff was so busy gazing at the grass, that he never noticed the big, green hairy hands gripping the sides of the bridge.

"Who's that tripping over MY bridge?" roared a terrible, rumbling voice.

Little Billy Goat Gruff stopped and stared at the green hairy hands. He gulped. "It is only I," he said, in a small squeaky voice, "a tiny little billy goat going to the grassy fields..."

"I'm coming to gobble you up!" roared the voice, and a huge and warty troll heaved himself onto the bridge.

"Oh no! Don't eat me," cried the little billy goat. "Why don't you wait for middle-sized Billy Goat Gruff? He's much bigger and fatter than me."

"Humph," said the troll. "You are tiny. No more than a snack really. Be off with you!"

Little Billy Goat Gruff scampered off the
bridge in a flash.

The troll hid under his bridge, and waited...

Soon, middle-sized Billy Goat Gruff came to
the river. His hooves went

TRIP-TRAP, TRIP-TRAP, TRIP-TRAP

as he trotted across the bridge.

"Who's that tripping over MY bridge?"
roared the troll.

"It's only me," said middle-sized Billy Goat
Gruff, in his not-so-squeaky voice. "I'm going to
the grassy fields to make myself round and fat."

"I'm coming to gobble you up!" said the troll,
and he leaped onto the bridge.

Middle-sized Billy Goat Gruff looked at the
troll and started to quiver and quake.

"Oh no!" he cried. "Why don't you wait until big Billy Goat Gruff comes? He's much bigger and fatter than me."

"Humph!" said the troll, crouching back under the bridge. "I've waited this long, I suppose I can wait a little longer. But this billy goat had better be *really* fat and *really* juicy!"

"Oh yes," said middle-sized Billy Goat Gruff.

"Be off with you, then," said the troll, and middle-sized Billy Goat Gruff ran.

The troll licked his lips and waited…

Soon there was a

TRIP-TRAP, TRIP-TRAP,

TRIP-TRAP

much louder than before.

The whole bridge creaked and groaned under big Billy Goat Gruff's great weight.

The troll smiled. "This is going to be a very tasty meal," he thought.

"Who's that tramping over MY bridge?" he roared, as he leaped onto the bridge.

"It is I! Big Billy Goat Gruff!" said the billy goat, in his great gruff voice.

"I'm going to gobble you up!" cried the troll.

"Oh no you're not," retorted Big Billy Goat Gruff. He stamped his hooves and reared up.

Then he flew at the troll, horns lowered, and with a mighty BAM, tossed him into the water.

The troll landed with an enormous SPLASH! He grunted and groaned and waved his fists furiously. But there was nothing he could do. He was swept down the rushing river.

As for the billy goats, they spent the rest of their days in the grassy meadows, growing round and fat and happy. The huge and warty troll was never seen again.

And so...

Snip, snap, snout, this tale's told out.

MOUSE DEER AND THE CROCODILE

M ouse Deer was oh so thirsty
as he ran down to the river
to drink. But could he? Or was
Crocodile lurking there?

51

He listened to the sounds of the jungle – the chattering monkeys, the croaking frogs. But no sound came from the river. "Perhaps it's safe..." thought Mouse Deer, creeping closer to the water on his tiny pointy hooves.

Then he remembered how still and silent Crocodile could be. "I'll just make sure," Mouse Deer decided...

He cleared his throat. "I wonder if the water's warm," he said, as loudly as he could. He picked up a long stick and dipped the tip into the water.

CHOMP! Crocodile's jaws grabbed hold of the stick and yanked it.

"Hee hee!" laughed Mouse Deer. "Don't you know a stick from a leg, Mr. Crocodile?"

Crocodile spat out the stick. His cold eyes stared at Mouse Deer. "I'll get you next time," he snapped.

Mouse Deer put his nose in the air and danced away, singing,

I'm a Mouse Deer,
Clever as can be,
Ha! Mr. Crocodile,
You can't catch me!

Mouse Deer skipped through the forest, nibbling on leaves and splashing in puddles, but soon he longed to drink again from the wide, wide river. Was Crocodile still there?

Mouse Deer looked left,
Mouse Deer looked right.
Nothing was in the river,
he decided. Just an
old log, floating on
the surface. At last,
he could drink!
Then Mouse Deer
remembered –
Crocodile looked
like a log when
he floated.

"I'll just make sure..." he decided.

Mouse Deer cleared his throat. "If that log is really Crocodile, it won't talk. But if it's only a log, it will tell me."

A deep, gravelly voice, like the sound of grinding stones, replied, "I'm only a log."

Mouse Deer laughed. "I've tricked you twice now, Mr. Crocodile. Do you really think a log can talk?" And he skipped away, singing his teasing song,

> *I'm a Mouse Deer,*
> *Clever as can be,*
> *Ha! Mr. Crocodile,*
> *You can't catch me!*

Crocodile was furious. "I won't let him trick me again," he swore. And he did what crocodiles do best – he waited.

It wasn't long before Mouse Deer came back. He wasn't thirsty now, but he was yearning to eat the tasty, juicy, succulent fruit on the other side of the river.

The trouble was, he'd be chomped by Crocodile if he tried to swim across. Unless…

"Oh Mr. Crocodile!" Mouse Deer called out.

Crocodile gave a toothy grin.

"Good afternoon, Mouse Deer," he said. "Have you come to be eaten at last? You'd make a wonderful snack."

Mouse Deer shook his head. "I have orders from the King," he announced.

"From the King?" asked Crocodile.

"Oh yes," said Mouse Deer. "He always gives his most important orders to me."

"And what exactly does the King want?"

"He wants me to count all crocodiles. Today! You must line up from this side of the river to the other."

"Well if it's for the King," said Crocodile. "Of course I'll do it."

He called to his friends and family and they lined up neatly across the river, just like a floating bridge.

"Stay as still as you can," ordered Mouse Deer. "We mustn't get this wrong for the King."

Mouse Deer jumped onto Crocodile's back. "One!" he called.

He jumped onto the next crocodile. "Two!" And the next. "Three!"

Mouse Deer kept jumping until he jumped all the way to the other side of the river.

"How many are there?" asked Crocodile.

"Just enough to get me across," said Mouse Deer with a smile. "I've tricked you again, Mr. Crocodile!" And he skipped away to eat the juicy fruits, singing,

I'm a Mouse Deer,
Clever as can be,
Ha! Mr. Crocodile,
You'll never catch me!

CHICKEN LICKEN

There was once a little chicken
with a wild imagination.
His name was Chicken Licken
and he lived on a farm.

While the other farm animals felt happy and safe, Chicken Licken saw danger at every turn. He'd see a shadow and think it was a three-eyed monster, or hear the tractor's engine and think it was a fire-breathing dragon.

One day, Chicken Licken was standing nervously near a towering oak tree, wondering if it was actually a fearsome ogre. Suddenly an acorn fell from the tree and hit him.

BONK!

"Ouch!" yelped Chicken Licken, looking up. He didn't see the acorn. Instead, he saw the sky above.

"The sky is falling!" he cried in a panic. "I must tell the King." And he raced off.

"Out of my way!" he called as he passed Henny Penny by the hen house.

"Whatever's the matter?" clucked the hen.

"The sky is falling!" cried Chicken Licken.

"Oh no," she gasped. "What shall we do?"

"I'm going to tell the King," announced Chicken Licken.

"Then I'll come too," Henny Penny replied.

They raced on together and met Cocky Locky, the rooster.

"What's going on?" he asked.

"The sky is falling!" cried Chicken Licken. "We're going to tell the King."

"Then I'll come too," Cocky Locky replied.

They rushed on past the duck pond.

"What's up?" quacked Ducky Lucky.

"The sky is falling!" cried Chicken Licken. "We're going to tell the King."

"Then I'll come too," Ducky Lucky replied.

On they sped, past the old barn where Goosey Loosey sat on her nest.

"What's happening?" she called out.

"The sky is falling!" cried Chicken Licken. "We're going to tell the King."

"Then I'll come too," Goosey Loosey replied.

They ran into the field where Turkey Lurkey was pecking for worms.

"What's all the fuss?" he asked.

"The sky is falling!" cried Chicken Licken. "We're going to tell the King."

"Then I'll come too," Turkey Lurkey replied.

And on they ran, deep into the royal forest: Chicken Licken, Henny Penny, Cocky Locky, Ducky Lucky, Goosey Loosey and Turkey Lurkey.

Watching them, from the shadow of an oak tree, was cunning Foxy Loxy.

"Whatever's the matter?" he asked.

"The sky is falling!" cried Chicken Licken. "We're going to the palace to warn the King," added Turkey Lurkey. "Is that right?" asked Foxy Loxy. "Then I'll show you a shortcut."

He pointed down a tunnel and the animals rushed inside. Oh no – a dead end! And there was Foxy Loxy, baring his teeth at the entrance.

"This isn't the way to the palace..." said Henny Penny.

"No," snarled Foxy Loxy. "This is where I keep my DINNER!"

Just then, the terrified animals saw an acorn fall from the tree and hit Foxy Loxy BONK on his head.

"Ouch!" said Foxy Loxy. He didn't see the acorn. Instead, he looked up in horror. "The sky really is falling," he cried, and ran off into the forest.

The other animals sighed with relief, then looked sternly at Chicken Licken.

"Do you still think we need to warn the King?" asked Goosey Loosey.

"Um, no," said Chicken Licken. "Sorry about that."

And they chased him all the way home.

THE MUSICIANS OF BREMEN

O nce upon a time, a cruel farmer wanted to get rid of his tired old donkey. "I'll run away," decided the donkey, "and become a musician."

So he set off down the road to
the city of Bremen, to join the
town band. On his way he met a
hunting dog, collapsed in a sorry heap.
"What's the matter?" asked the donkey.

"I've run away from my master,"
sighed the dog. "He wanted to
shoot me because I'm too old
to hunt. So I escaped, but now
I have nowhere to go."

"Why not come to Bremen with me?" the
donkey suggested. "I'm going to be a musician.
You can play the drums while I play the piano."

"What a good idea!" said the dog.

And the pair walked on,
thinking up tunes. They hadn't
gone far when they met a
bedraggled cat.

"What's the matter?" asked the donkey.

"My mistress tried to drown me," spat the cat, "because I've grown too old to chase mice. All I want is a quiet life by the kitchen stove, but she won't have it."

"Then come with us!" said the dog.

"We're going to be musicians in Bremen," explained the donkey. "I'm going to play the piano, Dog is going to play drums and I bet you'd make an excellent violinist."

The cat thought this was a brilliant plan, and padded along beside them.

It was getting dark as they neared a farm. Perched on the barn roof was a rooster, crowing at the top of his voice.

COCK-A-DOODLE-DOOOOOOOOOO!

"Why are you crowing now?" asked the donkey. "It's night-time, not morning."

"I'm going to be roasted for dinner tomorrow," sobbed the rooster. "Tonight is my last night."

"It doesn't have to be," said the donkey. "Run away with us. We're going to be musicians in Bremen."

"You can be our singer," said the cat.

"Lead the way!" said the rooster, and the four animals set off together.

Soon they reached a shadowy forest.

"Let's stay here tonight," said the donkey.

"I'm starving," moaned the dog.

"I'm freezing," shivered the cat.

The rooster flew to the top branch of a tree. "Hang on," he called, "I can see a light up ahead. Maybe someone lives there?"

The animals followed the light and found a curious house among the trees.

The donkey crept closer and peered in at the window.

"I see a table of food!" he said in excitement. "And a band of robbers," he added in dismay.

"I have an idea..." whispered the cat.

They huddled closer to hear her plan. Then the dog climbed on the donkey, the cat climbed on the dog, the rooster climbed on the cat and, when the cat said, "Now!" they all burst into song.

The robbers were so startled by the cacophony, they jumped up and raced out of the door without looking back.

The animals couldn't believe their luck. There was roast beef for the dog, fresh bread for the rooster, baked fish for the cat and a whole chocolate cake for the donkey. Happy and full at last, the animals blew out the candles and lay down to sleep.

But the robbers hadn't gone far. They were hiding in the trees, waiting for a chance to come back.

As the house went quiet and dark, the chief robber turned to the littlest member of the gang.

"Go and see who's stolen our hideout," he ordered gruffly.

All was still as the little robber tiptoed into the dark kitchen. He saw the cat's eyes gleaming and thought they were burning coals in a fireplace. "Just what I need," he murmured. He poked his candle at the coals, hoping to light it.

"AIIIEEEEK!" squealed the cat, leaping up and scratching the intruder.

Terrified, the robber ran to the back door and tripped over the dog, who snapped at him.

"Ouch!"

He hobbled into the yard where he was bucked by the donkey.

"Owwwww!"

This woke the rooster, who gave a deafening

COCK-A-DOODLE-DOO from the rooftop.

Scared out of his mind, the robber shot back into the forest.

"Quick!" he shouted to the other robbers. "We must get out of here. I've just been scratched by a witch, stabbed on the leg, hit with a club, and now an evil voice is yelling, 'Catch that rascal do!'"

The band of robbers turned and fled, and never returned to the house in the forest.

As for the animals, they never did become musicians. They didn't even make it to Bremen. They liked their new home so much, they decided to stay – and there they lived happily, for the rest of their lives.

THE HARE AND THE TORTOISE

It was March, and Hare had gone mad. He was springing through the air like a wild thing, bashing down daffodils and leaping over grassy hills.

The other animals watched in wonder.

"Bonkers," said the mole.

"Bananas," chattered the caterpillars.

"A crazy crazed crazy thing," laughed the lop-eared rabbits.

"Not I! Not I!" said Hare, bounding up to them, boxing the air with his fists. "It's Spring! Can't you feel it? I'm bounding with energy. Bursting with life."

Tortoise shook his head. "Here we go again," he muttered. "He's the same every year – full of talk, and it gets him nowhere."

"Nonsense," snapped Hare. "I'm in my prime. I could do anything. Run to the moon and back before you could creep across this field."

"I think not," said Tortoise. "You're like a bag of hot air. All puff, no substance."

"Is that a challenge?" cried Hare.

"If you want it to be," Tortoise sighed.

"Then a race it shall be!" Hare jumped joyously in the air. "First to the oak tree and back. *On your marks, get set, GO!*"

And he was off, bursting forward like a furry rocket. Tortoise rolled his eyes and plodded after him.

"Poor old Tortoise," said Mole. "He'll never win."

Hare made it to the oak tree in no time. He turned back and saw Tortoise, a speck in the distance, going PLOD, PLOD, PLOD...

"Ha!" laughed Hare. "No contest there. I might as well lie down and rest."

He curled up under the oak tree and promptly fell fast asleep.

PLOD, PLOD, PLOD went Tortoise, past the oak tree and back across the field. He moved very slowly, but he never stopped.

As the sun began to set, he neared the finish line. "Come on, Tortoise!" cheered the other animals.

Their voices carried on the wind and Hare woke with a start. "What's this? What's this?" he said, looking around. Then he spotted Tortoise. "Noooo!" he wailed. Using every muscle he possessed, he zipped across the field, tearing towards the finish line like the wind.

But he was too late. Tortoise was already there. "Just as I remarked," said Tortoise. "You're all talk. Slow and steady wins the race, you see."

THE UGLY DUCKLING

Crack! Crack! Peep, peep, peep, peep! One by one, Mother Duck's eggs were bursting open. One... two... three... four fluffy little ducklings came tumbling out.

"Aren't you perfect!" clucked Mother Duck. "Just one more to go." She turned and looked impatiently at the last egg. It was huge, much larger than the others, and rather dull and mottled. "Hmm," said Mother Duck. "Well, I suppose I'd better wait for you too."

As the sun was going down, the last egg finally began to break. Out crept the duckling. "Oh dear!" gasped Mother Duck. The duckling was very large, and very ugly.

The other ducks came over to see.

"Looks like a turkey chick to me," said an old duck. "Take it for a swim and see if it sinks."

So early the next morning, Mother Duck waddled down to the river, her four little fluffy ducklings following on behind. The Ugly Duckling came last, looking forlorn, his head bent low. "Turkey chick! Turkey chick!" chanted his brothers and sisters.

When they reached the water, Mother Duck watched as they all jumped in. Splish! Splosh! Splish! Splosh! SPLASH! Mother Duck held her breath, but all five bobbed back up again. "So he's not a turkey chick," thought Mother Duck. "Just a *very* ugly duckling."

Everyone else thought so too. The turkey in the farmyard gobbled at him. The farm girl tried to shoo him away. The farm dog barked; the farm cat hissed.

His brothers and sisters just laughed at him.
"You're the ugliest duckling we've *ever* seen!"
"I'll fly away," decided the Ugly Duckling.
"I'll fly away and never come
back." He flapped his little
wings and flew over the
farmyard fence. The gusty
wind swept him on and
on. He soared over
rivers and lakes until,
at last, exhausted, he
flopped down on a wild
and boggy moor.

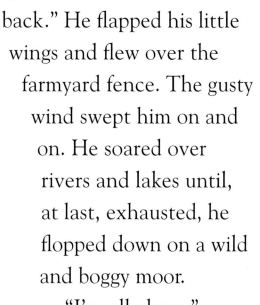

"I'm all alone,"
sniffed the Ugly
Duckling. "But at least
there's no one to laugh at
me here."

And he tucked his head under his wing.

BANG! BANG! Shots tore through the air. The Ugly Duckling looked up and squawked as two wild ducks fell down beside him. A great hunt was going on. The moors were suddenly alive with men, stalking along with guns, hunting dogs bounding beside them.

The Ugly Duckling crouched low among the grasses but a terrible dog had smelled him. He thrust his great black nose at the duckling, sniffed... and went on. "I am so ugly even a dog won't eat me," thought the Ugly Duckling.

On shaking wings, the Ugly Duckling flew on once more, until he came to a large lake. It was empty and glassy, silent and still.

"I'll live here," decided the Ugly Duckling.

He passed a lonely summer, watching and waiting as the leaves turned to orange and gold. As winter approached, the wind caught the leaves as they fell, and danced them on the frosty air.

One evening, just as the sun was setting, a flock of beautiful birds flew out of the bushes. The duckling had never seen anything like them before. They were swans, with long and graceful necks and glorious white wings, spread out across the sky.

The Ugly Duckling stretched out his neck towards them and uttered a cry so strange that it frightened him.

Then winter came. The ice on the lake froze so fast he was nearly trapped. The Ugly Duckling dragged himself out and collapsed on the newly fallen snow.

"I don't want to be alone," he thought. He watched the swirling snowflakes in the misty sky, remembering the beautiful birds.

The winter seemed to last forever, until one morning, the Ugly Duckling woke to feel the warm sun on his feathers. He heard the lark singing. Spring had come at last!

He flapped his wings and they felt sure and strong. He plunged into the lake, just as three swans came sailing by. The Ugly Duckling waited for them to laugh at him. He bowed his head in shame. But there... what was that in the water. Was it really his own reflection? The Ugly Duckling looked and looked again. It really was! He was a swan!

The other swans swam around him, wings outstretched in greeting. They rubbed his neck. They stroked his feathers. The Ugly Duckling was filled with joy.

"If only I'd known," he thought, "if only I'd guessed, when I was an Ugly Duckling, that one day I'd be as happy as this."

About the Stories

People all over the world have always enjoyed hearing stories about animals and imagining their adventures.

Over two thousand years ago, a Greek man named Aesop made up lots of animal fables. Each fable had a moral, or a lesson at the end. The Country Mouse learns that a quiet, simple life can be happier than a luxurious one. And Hare learns that you don't always win a race just by being fast.

Many traditional tales, such as *The Three Little Pigs* and *Mouse Deer and the Crocodile*, have been passed down through the generations from our grandparents' grandparents. We don't know who first made them up, but we like the stories so much that we keep on telling them.

Two brothers in Germany, Jacob and Wilhelm Grimm, were famous for their collection of folk tales, first published in 1812. That's where our version of *The Musicians of Bremen* comes from, although it had probably been told for many years before then.

A decade later in Denmark, Hans Christian Andersen was writing his own stories, including *The Ugly Duckling*. He wrote adult books too, but he's best known for his spellbinding fairy tales.

Rudyard Kipling wrote a wonderful book, published in 1902, called the *Just So Stories*. It is full of amusing, inventive tales of how elephants and other animals became the way they are.

If you enjoy these stories and share them with others, who knows? People may still be telling them hundreds of years from now.

Edited by Lesley Sims

Designed by Caroline Spatz

First published in 2013 by Usborne Publishing Ltd., Usborne House,
83-85 Saffron Hill, London EC1N 8RT, England. www.usborne.com
Copyright © 2013 Usborne Publishing Ltd.